Ice's Icing

Heroes for Hire, Book 20

Dale Mayer

ICE'S ICING: HEROES FOR HIRE, BOOK 20
Dale Mayer
Valley Publishing Ltd.

Copyright © 2019

ISBN-13: 978-1-773362-81-6
Print Edition

Books in This Series:

About This Book

Ice wanted only one thing in her life, and that was Levi—and maybe someone who was a blend of both of them. When he asked her to marry him, she was thrilled, but now she's struggling to pin down a wedding date for fear he'd been caught up in the moment and didn't really want to go through with it. When the compound is attacked, and they are forced to go on the offense, she realizes what's truly important.

Levi is infuriated that Ice refuses to set a wedding date. He's always loved her, and there will never be anyone else for him. This fact is reinforced as they come under attack by a military group trying to overthrow a government that he aided.

As the bullets fly and the body count mounts, who says you can't have your cake and your icing too!

Chapter 1

CELITE DANNING SPUN on her heels and walked away from Levi. It was hard to do, but she was getting better at it.

He reached out, grabbed her arm and spun her around again, his face twisted with anger. "What do you mean, *no?*" he roared. "I asked you to marry me. You said yes, but, anytime I try to set a date, you keep pushing it off. Why?"

Ice stood firm, her hands on her hips. "You're not ready," she snapped.

"It's not for you to tell me when I'm ready or not," he said, his voice gentle as he stared at her searchingly.

She smiled up at him. "No, it isn't. But it's a momentous time. And I don't want you to make a mistake."

His eyebrows shot up at that. He crossed his arms and said, "Really? You're telling me that I don't know what I want?"

"*Really?*" she said, mimicking him. "Of course you don't know what you want. You're a man." She laughed.

He reached out, snagged her up and kissed her hard. Immediately passion swept over them, as it always did. He held her close, murmuring against her ear, "Ever since I asked you, I've been trying to set a date. Please put me out of my misery."

"Okay," she said, "but I want to think about it. An awful

lot of people live and work here with us, and we're likely to start something."

He winced at that but bravely said, "Maybe we should do a group wedding then, like Badger's crew did."

She shook her head. "I don't think that'll work. We only got caught up in that one because of other people's plans. That's not something we do here."

"Maybe that's a good thing," he said. "I have to admit, I was a little concerned about that."

She chuckled. "I'm sure you were. But the bottom line is, a group wedding is not a good idea here."

"So what do you want to do?"

She frowned. "I know Bailey and Alfred will want to do the cooking. I don't want anybody else here but family and friends. I want my father to give me away."

"What about Bullard?"

She stared up at Levi. "I would love that, but I don't know if you would."

He gave her that lazy sexy smile she adored. "Sweetheart, I don't mind in the least. But I don't know if Bullard would want to come."

"Then we'll leave it to Bullard to decide," she said. "He's a very good friend, as are many of his people. I wouldn't want to exclude them."

"In that case, you just doubled the numbers."

She scrunched up her face and shuddered.

He leaned closer and said, "Maybe you're the one getting cold feet."

Heat flashed between them again, and she shook her head. "No cold feet here. I can think of nothing I want more than to be your wife."

At that, he kissed her again, but, just as they were deepening their kiss, the alarm sounded throughout the compound. They broke apart and bolted in different directions. Ice headed for the control room, and Levi headed downstairs to the garage. In the control room, Stone watched the cameras. She stepped inside, and he said, "Lock the door behind you."

She closed and locked it and hit the security button. "What's going on?"

"I'm not sure," Stone said, "but I counted two gunmen with semiautomatic rifles outside."

Ice gasped and sat down. The sirens were still going off outside. The pool had just opened. Likely half-a-dozen people were out there, but everybody had been briefed on the alarms. At the first sound, everybody needed to be inside and locked down in the compound. It also meant all the men and their partners should be armed and ready for full-on warfare. Ice hated the fact that she and the others had to live in a war zone, but it was what it was.

And she'd rather live in *this* war zone than continue the work she used to do in a different one. She counted on everybody here to do their jobs. No way would she let something like this stop her from taking the next step in her life.

"There." Stone tapped one of the monitors.

She glanced at it just in time to see a flash from a scope. She nodded. "Let me talk to Levi."

"He's on the PA system now," Stone said.

"Levi, two onscreen. One shooter up on the back quarter atop the ridge. Back camera is still working. He doesn't appear to know. We have a second shooter outside our secret door."

"Okay," Levi said, his voice calm and controlled. "We've

got two teams of men going out. My team will take the secret door, and we've got another team going out through the back."

"Anybody going out the back is likely to get picked off by the sniper," Stone said.

"Maybe," Levi said, "but not if we get there first. We'll have to come up with an alternate way to get on the other side of that hill without having to go around it."

"You want to bore a tunnel through there?" Ice asked.

"Talk about spending some money," Levi said.

"I don't care," Ice said. "I don't want anything to compromise our security."

"We'll talk about it afterward. Make sure everybody is accounted for. Do a full roll call, and anybody who's off-base needs to be told they can't come home."

"Will do," Ice said. It was standard procedure. All the women had been thoroughly briefed before they moved onto the compound, but they hadn't had an incident in months. One of the reasons they always had to do these practice sessions was just to keep everybody up-to-date with safety procedures.

With Stone manning the security systems, Ice headed down to get a headcount. She went to the physical roster on the kitchen wall and checked to see who was on and who was off. On the chalkboard beside her, she added up all the partners and started making calls. Ten minutes later, she had two people running errands in town, seven at work at their various jobs in town and the rest were on the base, locked into their apartments. All of them wanted to come back to the main compound building. Ice sent the message that nobody was to move yet.

As she studied the layout of the compound, she said,

"Alfred, we really do need a secure way for them to get from the individual apartments to the main building."

"Yes," he said, "that's that tunnel we were talking about."

"And we need a way to get on the other side of the hill. That's the second time we've been caught by that blind spot."

"We can have cameras set up that keep that blind spot from being blind, but we can't get there if a sniper settles in first."

"Exactly," she said. "I've contacted everybody, and we need to open the house in town, in case those currently there have to stay. Seven at work and two shopping."

"So, nine women?" Bailey said, coming out of the pantry.

"Yes, but Flynn is here working, and Anna's at her place. We've also got Logan in town, so he can help with the women."

"We'll probably need a couple more men."

"Harrison and Easton are out there that we can call on," Ice said. "I want them to get to the safe house with the women too." She picked up the phone and made the calls.

"Do we have any idea what's going on?" Alfred asked.

"The usual. This time we have a sniper. We're looking to see if he is connected to a team."

"There'll be a team," Alfred said comfortably. "I just wonder who and what's behind it."

"I don't know. I'm getting damn tired of it though."

"It's to be expected," Alfred said. "Doing good work pisses off the wrong people."

She just rolled her eyes at him.

As he walked back to the kitchen island, he said, "I think

I'll put on some cinnamon buns. People will need the extra boost."

"I'll help," Bailey said.

Ice watched as two of her favorite team members headed to the pantry. Of course it didn't hurt that they were forever bringing out wonderful things for everyone to eat. It was certainly needed regardless, but especially at crunch time.

She sat with a notepad and wrote down all the things she needed to keep track of. As the company got bigger, the logistics got harder. She had lots of staff working in the office now as well, not to mention most of them were partners to the men working the ops for the company. It would seem to be the prudent way to keep everybody happy, but, at the moment, Levi questioning their personal life had pushed her into a territory she wasn't comfortable with. It wasn't that she was holding back on setting a wedding date, it was all about not wanting to have him regret it.

That he'd actually asked her had completely blown her away. She figured he'd been caught up in the wedding thralls of Badger and his group. Then she figured it was hard for Levi to do anything *but* ask her. At the same time, when this shit was going on all around them, she had to wonder just what was the priority here? Her safety and that of everyone was the priority, not getting a chance to walk down an aisle. She didn't even want that. She just wanted to get married out by her own pool, on her own compound, with her father handing her off to Levi.

And she knew Levi would be all for that type of ceremony.

She was totally okay to bring in anybody from Badger's group, any of their friends out of California or even any of Bullard's group out of Africa. Bullard in particular. He was a special friend, and they had a connection she hadn't had with many others. But, if Bullard struggled with the idea of her finally tying the knot with Levi, then her relationship with Bullard could become hellish. Yet she and Bullard had come to an agreement a long time ago. He knew perfectly well; Levi was her partner in all ways. So why the hell was she taking umbrage over Levi trying to set a wedding date? She got up and walked over to the secret entrance directly into the compound, not at all happy that she hadn't heard from anybody. She hit the PA system and called out, "Stone?"

"The team outside the secret entrance is clear," he said. "Waiting on the team heading for the blind spot."

"Good enough," she said. "I'll send out two teams by road. We need to know where these guys are coming from and what they're after."

"Let me do another satellite search first," he said. "I was there a few moments ago, and it was clear, but give me another second."

She waited as she walked out to the massive garage, the two teams waiting in their vehicles for the go sign. When they saw her, Evan leaned over and said, "Have you got the word yet?"

"Just waiting on Stone to do another satellite search. Levi's taken out two at the secret entrance, but we still have one sniper up on the blind spot."

"If there're three, chances are good more are around," the men in the trucks called out.

She nodded and opened the garage doors. "Stone?"

"They're clear. One head south. A vehicle's parked in the trees about half a mile down."

She relayed that back to Dakota. He nodded and drove

out, heading to the left.

Merk was driving the second truck. She faced him and said, "You need to go to the right and drive straight ahead for another four miles, according to Stone."

Just then Stone's voice came over her phone again. "Make that five," he said. "It's on the move. A black Jeep, open back, with one driver who looks like he's got a lot of weapons in the front seat."

Merk gave a hard grin and said, "We're on it. Five miles is nothing."

"Do you have a third spot?" Ice asked. "I've got a third truck ready to go. Jace is driving."

"He'll follow Merk," Stone said, his voice cool. "But at the first T, he's heading left. Looks like we've got a couple vans sitting there. I think that's the communication system."

"Then he's not going alone," she said. She walked over to Rhodes and said, "I'm taking another vehicle with you."

The men split up as she hopped into the driver's side and turned on the engine. "Stone, I'm heading out too. Keep watch on the satellite."

"Always," he said. "I'll tell Levi."

She chuckled. "You better not tell him until I'm gone. Do you know what he'll say?"

"He'll say, *That damn woman had better marry me soon,*" Stone said. "When will you put him out of his misery?"

"Soon," she promised. "But I just want a family party. I don't want anything big and formal."

"We're a big family as it is," Stone said, laughing, "but I'm really glad to ditch the formalwear."

"We'll talk when I'm back."

"SHE WHAT?" LEVI yelled into the PA system. "Stone, really?"

"She didn't want Jace heading to the communication base on his own," he said. "She figured two vehicles would be better."

"That might be," Levi said, "but that doesn't mean she should have gone herself."

"Whoever planned this attack didn't think it through. Normally we have half this number of men at home."

"I know," Levi said. "We've got the first three prisoners in the jail cell. Nobody's conscious."

"Any IDs?"

"Nothing. Black-ops all the way. Top military-grade equipment, clothing. No tattoos that we could see either."

"Chips?" Stone asked.

"We're running scanners on them right now," Levi said. "Have you kept the eyes in the sky on the four vehicles?"

"Yes, and all four appear to be engaged."

"Shit," Levi said, striding toward the garage. He opened the internal door, stepped out and saw all four of the military vehicles they kept were gone. He headed to his truck. "Where do I need to be?"

"Looks like trouble with Ice," Stone said soberly. "Take your men and head right out to the first junction, then you head left. Less than three miles."

"Switching over to comm," Levi said, "you're now on my headset." He ordered his team outside to the trucks. With two vehicles racing down the road, he was ready to have some very strong words with Ice. He knew it wasn't fair, but he wanted to keep her safe. And he knew she'd fight him every step of the way because she would want to keep him safe as well.

The trouble was, they were partners for a reason, and she would never be the little woman who stayed home. He loved her for it, but, damn, the last thing he wanted was to have her injured.

When they were about a mile out, his headset crackled. "You're coming up on the four vehicles," Stone said. "There's been no movement since Ice arrived."

"In that case, I'm pulling over early," Levi said.

"Pull up right now," Stone said urgently.

Levi pulled off the road and into a group of trees. It was a rough landing, but the other vehicle pulled up beside him. "What have you got?"

"Looks like Ice is being taken prisoner. They're walking her toward you now. One hundred yards ahead."

"Are they holding rifles on her?"

"Yes," Stone said. "Get moving now."

Levi's men ran, loaded for bear. As they came around the bend, sure enough, Ice and Jace stood with their backs turned, and two men held rifles on them.

Levi didn't even think about it. He raised his handgun and fired one shot. He took down the first shooter with a bullet right between the eyes. When it came to this kind of game, absolutely no way would he shoot to injure. When the other gunman was shot down a second later, the place erupted with return fire from the nearby roadsides. His men raced for cover. Ice, on the other hand, dove backward, grabbed the gunman's weapon and, from her crouching position, started firing.

Yeah, that was his Ice.

Amid the gunfire, he ran to her, helped her to her feet and said, "You stand guard over these guys. I want that one alive, if he survives, and this one, well, he faced a death sentence the minute he pulled a gun on you." The gunfire slowed.

"Go, go, go," she said, "there're several more."

He shot her a disbelieving look, but his men had already spread out and had quickly taken the rest hostage. Before long, he and Ice stood facing the newest group of prisoners. They were all dressed the same as the ones he'd already rounded up. None spoke, only glared at them, murder in their eyes.

Levi said to Ice, "We've taken down the three at the compound, and we've got seven hostages here, two down and several more vehicles. I don't have a clue what's going on or why."

"I know," she said. "We haven't had an attack like this in forever."

"Yeah. We need to get to the bottom of it—and fast."

But, from the looks of it, nobody would talk. Levi walked away, out of earshot, and hit his headset. "Stone, we've got this under control, two down and seven prisoners. We'll bring them in under their own power, then sedate them. What the hell's happening with Merk and Dakota?"

"Merk's taken over the vehicle full of weapons to the north, has one prisoner down and tied up, and he's looking for the second one. With those two we've got a dozen prisoners. As for Dakota, he's still chasing the other vehicle."

"Do we still think it's involved, or maybe it's a decoy?"

"No way to tell, but he's not giving up."

Levi nodded. "It's not like Dakota—or any of the men—to give up with something like this. Never."

He motioned to all the captives and called out to his men, "Have them taken back to the compound. All the vehicles go too." Levi's men split up, bound the shooters, securely placing hoods over their heads, then loaded them up. All the vehicles slowly progressed back to the compound. It wasn't very far, and, once they were all inside, Levi sent two more men after Merk. "Help him bring the two gunmen and their vehicle back."

As soon as this second round of captives were inside the compound, Levi locked the main gate to the compound, knowing Merk and Dakota would get back in again on their own. "Stone, we're in."

"I saw you," he said. "I think Merk's okay, but it didn't hurt to double up on the manpower there."

"I just don't get this," Levi said. His voice was harsh as he watched the men being unloaded. They were led down to the compound's jail and locked up in their own community cell—but not for long. Levi looked outside, swearing at them. Everyone had been searched and checked, but not one had an ID. He turned to his men and said, "Two on shifts steady. They're never to be left unguarded."

No one argued. The fact that this many had been involved in an attack on the compound was serious because everybody had somebody special here they were interested in protecting.

Levi headed upstairs to their bedroom, angry, fed up, wanting to get to the bottom of it. But, so far, he didn't have anything to go on.

Ice was up there pouring coffee and held one out to him. He took it, hating to see his hand shaking. She nodded, smiled and said, "I'm okay, you know?"

He leaned over, gave her a hard kiss and said, "You damn well better be."

She beamed a smile at him and said, "I don't get this. Why now?"

"I don't know. The problem is, we've pissed off a lot of people, and we've accumulated a lot of enemies. This one was way too organized."

"Like a miniwar," she said. "A lot of manpower, a lot of money and a lot of weaponry went into this."

"The men are doing a search on the vehicles. I'm heading back down there."

"I'm coming," she said. "Don't you worry. I'm coming too."

And the two walked downstairs to the garage to figure out what the hell was going on.

Chapter 2

ICE WATCHED AS Levi commanded the search of all the intruders' vehicles. They were waiting on Dakota, who had taken off after the first vehicle, and Merk, who was on the second one, the fully armed Jeep. Just then, Levi got a call from Stone. "Dakota's on his way back. He did stop the other vehicle but has determined they are not related to this incident. He's turned around and is coming back."

"Well, that would be nice for a change," Ice said.

Levi nodded his head, responding to Ice. "Good. So, what we've got is what we've got." Then he turned back to his phone. "Stone, do a full satellite sweep and see if anybody else is shaking out of the dirt up there. They might think, now we have everybody locked up and secure, that they can make a move to rescue their friends."

"I'll go up to security and take a look myself." Ice grabbed her coffee cup, turned to take a stroll by their captives in the compound's jail facilities. After processing each, the intruders were kept in single cells, set up like solitary confinement, with only eye slits to peer in or out of. Regardless the whole jail facility was under surveillance. She shook her head and headed upstairs. She gave a rap on the door to the control room and told Stone, "Let me in."

"The least you could have done was brought me a cinnamon bun and a coffee," he said in an aggrieved tone.

"Go get your own," she said as she sat down. "I want to make sure nothing's happening on a wider satellite search."

"I've already got it running. I don't know what's going on, but this is big."

"It's too big," Ice said. "It makes no sense. Who the hell have we pissed off this time?"

Stone chuckled and said, "Everybody. Remember that old saying about being judged by your enemies?"

"Wouldn't it be nice if we didn't have to get judged at all? I'm getting fed up with this whole thing."

He smiled. "Well, you are, and you aren't. It's frustrating as hell to be under attack at our own home turf. Plus we haven't had an attack on the compound in a long time."

"I know," she said, "and I want to get to the bottom of it now, so I can sleep tonight."

"Especially so you get up again tomorrow morning to put our intrepid leader out of his misery."

"Ha," she said, "He's only half of the leaders' team."

"The thing is," Stone said quietly, "you're just as miserable. Because you want to be married to him as well."

She shot Stone a searching look.

He nodded and said, "We all know it. You were thrilled when you got engaged. So I'm not sure why you're trying to slow him down now."

"I'm afraid he was just caught up in the moment," she said slowly. "And I don't want to push him."

"In this case, you're better off to push him," Stone said. "Push him and lock it down. He's always been yours. You've always been his. You don't need a ceremony to make it official, but, as long as either of you want it, then you should do it and move on."

She chuckled. "I agree, but, for right now, we've got

more shit happening, and a wedding is not part of the program."

Stone gave her a secretive smile and said, "Maybe not. But just like Badger didn't have a clue what hit him, you might not be aware of what'll hit you." At that, he stood and said, "I'll leave you, our intrepid leader's other half, and go get my own coffee and a cinnamon bun."

Ice leaned back in her chair slowly. Badger was their friend, and his group wedding had been a hell of a lot of fun. But no way did she want to get blindsided like Badger had been. She understood why those women had done it, and Ice had agreed at the time to help with the secret marriages ceremony, but hers was a very different case here. She'd been wanting to get married since forever. Yet maybe Stone was right. Maybe it was time to stop looking for reasons not to and just get the job done.

LEVI HAD TWO of his men bring out the still-hooded prisoners one at a time. The hoods had to be removed for photos to run facial recognition programs on, but they were quickly replaced. The intruders were fingerprinted, checked for chips, cheeks swabbed, ear printed in a move similar to finger printed, and then moved to a different cell. There was complete silence—none of the prisoners made a sound as they were processed. Levi realized this was a well-trained group of men who were either expecting a huge payout or were terrified of doing something wrong and paying the ultimate price.

Except ... he didn't see fear in any of them, and that concerned him. A huge payout was hard to argue with. ... He didn't have a clue who could possibly be involved, but, as soon as he had the prisoners' data, Levi reached out to his contacts and ran fingerprints through as many databases as he could. One of the first people he contacted was Bullard. He reached out by phone and started sending images.

Bullard answered, "Can't a guy get any sleep?"

"When you're dead," Levi snapped. "We're in a full-on siege here. We've taken twelve prisoners, and we're not sure how many more are out there to take down."

Bullard snapped to attention. "That's a lot to take on the compound. What's up?"

"I don't know," Levi said. "Stone saw the first ones coming through our hidden cameras. They had several vehicles and a command station set up around the corner. But don't kid yourself, this isn't government-based, anybody's government. This is a full-on heavy-military op, with top-of-the-line gear, and no one's saying a word. They're well-trained."

"Interesting. Who'd you piss off?"

"Half the world," Levi said, cracking a grin. "You pissed off the other half."

"Well then, together we'll rule," Bullard said. In the background, Levi could hear him clicking buttons. "I'll run these faces through the database," he said, "but so far I'm not seeing any ..." His voice trailed off.

"What'd you find?"

"I have a hit on one. He's bad news. Private Soonson turned mercenary. Works for a private army out of Guatemala, which pays huge money, and they've been slowly building a bigger army."

"Through what source?"

"Mexico."

"These guys here are all white, although several are of European descent," Levi added.

"Yeah, I think we've got Juan, the Colombian drug lord, who's trying to get out of his family business and get into something a little more to his liking. I heard rumors the little shit had big plans. Guatemala is close enough for him to raise Cain. But then so are Mexico and several other countries."

"So why did Juan come here is the big question?" Levi said.

"You working for any South American governments right now?"

Levi closed his eyes and thought about it. "Four."

Bullard gave a bark of laughter. "Then I highly suggest you take a look at those four governments and see if this Columbian guy's got anything to do with them. His name's Juan Pickonous," he said. "Your guys all look like mercenaries."

"It's funny how they have a type, isn't it?" Levi said. "Stone-cold killers with dead eyes."

"Physically fit, lightning-fast reflexes, no family—or none they care about—and the only God they know is money."

"And power," Levi clarified. "Lots love their work because it's the only job that lets them terrorize and kill."

"Yep, fewer rules and a lot more leeway for shitty behavior."

"Okay, put your ear to the ground to see if you hear anything," Levi said. "My grocery bill is about to go through the roof just keeping these assholes here for the next few hours."

"You can expect a call pretty soon from this Juan character, if it's the guy I'm thinking of. He'll want his men back."

"And he can have them," Levi said in a harsh tone. "In a box."

He went to hang up when Bullard called out, "Hey, when's the wedding?"

"If I knew I'd tell you," Levi growled. This time he did hang up. The last thing he wanted was the wedding brought up again. He knew Bullard expected an invite, and Levi and Bullard appeared to be on good terms now that he'd finally accepted that Levi and Ice would be together forever.

Just then he got a text from Bullard.

Getting word something's happening in Guatemala. This Juan guy's involved.

Levi started tapping his sources. He could see this coming from Guatemala. A lot of big business for Legendary Security had happened thereabouts. Plus that country was a mess, but the wealthy were definitely getting wealthier, and that meant the rest of the peons were getting poorer. Prime for revolts. Levi hated to say it, but it was all too possible this unrest had led to his compound's siege.

He'd been working for the Argentinean government lately too, trying to find these terrorist cells intent on taking down their government. It looked as if maybe one of the groups from Guatemala had figured out what Levi was up to in Argentina and had come here to hit him at home—and the fact that they'd actually found him concerned Levi. He didn't like being blindsided, nor did he want anybody to have intel on his place.

If there was a way to hide his compound with stealth technology, he'd have paid for it ten times over.

But it wouldn't be available anytime soon.

So somebody had found out where he'd gone to ground and had decided to come after him. And that was fine. He was okay to have a few come after him.

But they wouldn't do it twice.

Chapter 3

ICE AND LEVI called a meeting in the kitchen. They'd left six men on guard downstairs in the jail facility and kept Stone stationed in the security room with Merk, adding extra eyes as they brought in more satellite feeds. With fresh coffee, Ice explained what was going on.

The men and women nodded but stayed quiet until Rhodes asked, "So we're going after them?"

"In a way, that's probably the best," Levi said. "But we have to take them out permanently one way or the other. Because, if we don't succeed, they'll come back again."

"Well, that's easy," Flynn said. "We always look after our home base first."

Levi nodded. "We'll also be short-staffed here, if I send out everyone who's due to go out next to hit back at these guys."

"They must have known that," Bailey said, standing against the corner, a cup of coffee in her hand.

"Exactly," Levi said, giving her a gentle smile. "But you'll be fine."

She shrugged. "I really don't give a shit. They come close to me or Alfred, I'll take the cast-iron frying pan to them."

That got a bark of laughter out of her partner, Dakota. He got up, kissed her soundly and snagged a cinnamon bun hiding behind her back. She tried to swat his hand, but he wasn't having anything to do with that. Dakota sat back down with a big grin and said, "So, we need eight men, or do we want to go in smaller?"

"Eight men," Ice said. "Four on the ground, four on the move. On the ground, it'll be backup teams, two plus two, to stay in touch with command at all times. And I think we'll need to bring in four more, just in case." She watched as everyone processed that strategy.

"If we go in too big," Flynn said with a cautionary tone, "that's not good either."

"I know," Levi said. "The bigger we are, the harder it is to hide. But we have to go in, and we have to go in hard and fast."

"None of these guys have anything on them. What do you want to do with them?" Flynn asked.

"I'd take them out and deep-six them," Dakota said. "But that won't work, so ... suggestions?"

"We can hardly turn them over to the local cops," Levi said. "They'll have themselves out in no time."

"Time to call in a couple favors from the brass," Flynn said.

Levi nodded. He turned to Ice, who was already busy writing notes. She waved her hand at him. "Keep talking. I know who I'll call. Don't you worry. The garbage will get taken out pretty damn fast."

"Do you need help with that?" Sienna asked.

Ice looked at her, smiled and said, "Maybe. I'll get your help in the office."

Sienna nodded, while the others went back to discussing how and what.

Ice listened with half an ear. She knew this was what had to happen, but she also hated that this had come home to them. Though it wasn't the first attack they'd had by any means, it was the largest. It was too much like a military operation. These men were well-trained.

"Or we use them as bait," she said suddenly and looked up.

Kai sat in the corner, looking at her with interest. "Or as a bartering chip."

Ice nodded. "We can take them back, dump them in their own backyard, incapacitated. Drug them for at least twenty-four hours, so we can go in and take care of business and get out again."

"But when they wake up," Dakota protested, "you know they'll come after us again."

"Maybe not," Levi said suddenly. "Where are their bank accounts? If we could take away what it is they really want, or at least let them know we can take away what they really want, chances are they won't come back."

"If we took away their paychecks," Kai said, "at least for now, … they won't work for nothing. Not this group of mercs. So, if there's no money, they'll just find another boss."

"Correct. Which means we have to take out their boss *and* stop the money from flowing."

"We need names. We need a location," Ice said calmly. "I'm taking several women up to the office. We'll get started." She stood and looked at Levi. "And, if you're going on this trip, you better make damn sure there's a spot for me too." And she marched out.

LEVI SHOOK HIS head. "I *am* going on this damn trip," he announced, "but she's not."

The group all raised an eyebrow, but no one said a word.

Levi groaned. "Except we'll need her helicopter skills, won't we?"

The men shrugged. Dakota said, "Unless you want to do a ground convoy. Depending on our destination, flying directly to Columbia would take like six hours one way. To Guatemala, more like three hours one way. But driving? ... Figure roughly a week, what with the border crossings. Unless we do a combo, driving partway, flying partway."

"We need to set up an operation, and it needs to be fast, and it needs to be now." They sat down and started on a plan, and, after a couple hours, the men switched guards with the six downstairs. Rhodes walked back there too, just to see them all for himself.

It was hard for Levi to imagine how he'd ended up with so many men working for him—well over twenty at any given time—but he had men already out on jobs right now, so that only left twelve on-site. He had another two men in town, on loan and looking after the women there. As soon as Levi got the all clear, he'd get them home to the compound.

Dakota added, "We have to make sure we hit them before they have time to send in reinforcements to break out their team."

"Exactly," Levi said. "We're going over the vehicles right now too. We need to make sure we've pulled out any intel we can."

"I think Stone was in there earlier, digging out the software they were running," Flynn said. "And I think Merk is in the garage, tearing the vehicles apart."

Just then the kitchen door opened, and Merk stuck his head in. "Levi, come look at this."

Levi and the others trooped out to the garage to one of

the vans the prisoners had used as a command center.

"Is this something you can rent?" one of the men asked from behind Levi.

Levi shook his head. "I wouldn't have thought so. But it looks like old military. I'd think they'd have something like this in the US if they're operating a cell of some kind here."

"And, if that's the truth," Dakota said, "we can probably get some government assistance too."

"We'll see how big this op gets," Levi said. "I'd like to keep this small and intense if we can. Much better if it's just us. Otherwise we have to deal with authority issues."

"Which is never fun," Merk said with a grin. He motioned at the inside of one of the vehicles and said, "They've got full satellite."

"Which makes no sense that they would get close enough so that we could get to them, much less capture them too," Flynn said.

"True," Levi said, not liking that thought at all. "A part of me worries this is a trap."

"Oh, it definitely was a trap," Merk said. "That's one of the things I wanted to show you."

Levi's eyebrows rose.

Merk brought Levi around to the side of the vehicle and bent low, pointing under the engine. "I disconnected two bombs—one on this side and one on the front."

Levi's breath sucked back tight against his chest. He could hear the same reaction from the others. He shook his head. "We never even thought of that, did we? We need to change protocol for next time."

"No," Merk said. "It's the first thing I did look for though. They didn't get a chance to detonate before being taken. The remotes were inside each cab. But, if even one of those guys got loose, … these were military-grade IEDs. *American* military grade."

Levi's mouth turned down at the corners. "Not like that's totally unexpected though," he said. "When you think about it, we have to deal with our weapons being sold on the black market all over the world."

"I know," Merk said. "Just sucks that it's sitting here on our own property."

"Did you go over all the vehicles?"

Merk shot him a look that basically told him that he'd asked a foolish question.

At that, Rhodes came up from where the prisoners were and said, "All the captives have been processed and are locked up separately. I want to make sure I'm part of anything happening up here."

Levi nodded. "This will be a big deal, but we'll be quiet and calm about it. Way too much shit is happening." Levi turned to Merk. "Any intel in the vehicles?"

"A lot of it. Going back for several months at least. Satellite images of here *and* their home base. They were trying to keep an eye on Columbia at the same time as they were keeping an eye on us here."

"Perfect," Levi said. "We need the location. We need an operation to get in and get out."

"Already working on it," Merk said. "Rhodes here will get the transport under control." He stopped, looked over at Levi and said, "What about Ice?"

"What about her?" Levi said.

"Is she coming? It determines whether we'll get a helicopter on the other end."

Levi swore and said, "Then I guess she's coming. But I wish she wasn't."

"Can't do that, boss," Rhodes said. "She's been at your side since the beginning. She'll be there at the end. Don't take that away from her."

"I know," he said, pinching the bridge of his nose. "I would just like to know she stays safe."

"And that's how she feels about you too," Rhodes said in a warning tone. "If she thinks you'll treat her like the little woman ..." He shook his head. "I can't imagine what she'll have to say about that."

"Let's just set it up," Levi said. "You've got twenty-four hours, and we have to decide what to do with the garbage we've collected around here. The live ones and their vehicles."

"I kind of liked Ice's idea of taking the prisoners back to where they came from," Merk said. "They're dead weight, and that's a problem, but otherwise we can call some of our network and see what they have for suggestions."

"I've got a suggestion," Flynn said, "but then you already know how I feel about it."

"We don't murder in cold blood," Levi reminded. "But we'll keep their weapons, their vehicles as spoils of war. After all, they were just gonna blow up these two vans anyway. We may need their vans on this op. We'll see as we firm up this plan."

The guys all agreed on those points.

"If we take the prisoners back," Dakota added, "they'll just get weaponized again, and we can shoot them down there."

"That way we don't have to bury them," Rhodes said without cracking a smile. With that, he got down to business.

Chapter 4

BACK IN THE office, Ice had the women working hard on getting the logistics sorted out. Ice made two calls, one to somebody within the government and one to somebody outside of the country. The government guy didn't want anything to do with her prisoners. She groaned. "You sure you don't want a dozen deliveries?"

"No, I don't," he said, "I don't want to know anything about it. Guatemala's bad news without adding in a Columbian takeover. We're not involved in any ups and downs there, and I don't want any of that coming back on American soil."

Ice snorted. "Too late," she said. "They are already here, and we have the mercs, the guns, the intel and the vehicles to confirm it."

There was silence for a long moment. "I'll get back to you." And he hung up.

Her next call was to a friend who was always there when she needed him. Then again it was reciprocal. When he heard her voice, he said, "You only call me in times of trouble. What's up?"

She gave him a shortened version of what had happened.

He whistled. "Yeah, I know who that guy is. He's trying to take over the world, one country at a time. He's starting with Guatemala, but he's from Mexico, part of one of the big

Colombian drug families down there, trying to branch out on his own. He's young. He's arrogant. He's beyond wealthy with a steady supply of more money coming in from the drug trade."

"Right. Anything you can do to help us out would be wonderful."

"Hate to touch Guatemala," he said.

"So do we—at least more than we have been," Ice said. "We've been helping that government, which is of course likely why we've been targeted. If this Juan character can take out everyone helping the Guatemalan government, then he's got an easier time of it taking over the country."

"Makes sense," he said. "You can have ten men. They're already there in Guatemala. Use them for backup only, please."

"Which side are they working for?"

He gave a bark of laughter. "The same side you are. We can't let this idiot get into power in Guatemala, or the whole world better watch out."

"That's the problem with too much money," Ice said quietly. "And the support is welcome. Thank you." When he hung up on her, she sat here for a long moment and then called command to check where Levi was.

Stone said he was in the garage at the vehicles, going over the intel they'd found. Stone warned her. "The vehicles also came in wired."

She sucked in her breath for a long moment and said, "I presume Merk found them?"

"Yeah, we should have checked them first. And the fact that we didn't …"

"I know. We got lazy," she said. "We'll have to get handhelds to run over every vehicle every time we go anywhere. Make sure they're standard issue in all the vehicles now."

"I'm on it," Stone said. "Kind of pissy that we're always looking over our shoulders. I thought by now, you know, I'd be getting married, have half-a-dozen kids."

"We always will be looking over our shoulders," she said sadly.

"Unless you guys want to get into a different line of business," Stone joked.

"I don't know about that. If I thought there was any other way to stop this from happening, I'd consider it. But, at the moment, when these assholes are always coming to take us out …"

"Hey, but just think. We did catch all of them. That's different from the way we started."

Ice smiled. "That's true enough, but just look at the danger having a family caused us. It makes us vulnerable."

"When you love, you're already vulnerable," Stone said, his voice gentling. "Just go and get married, will you? Levi would be a whole lot easier to live with. You too." And, on that note, he closed the comm on her.

She swore and stood to see the other women looking at her with raised eyebrows. She just glared at them. "I'll get married when I'm darn good and ready."

"Or when you're not so afraid," Sienna said.

Ice rounded on her, and then her shoulders sagged. "Is it wrong to be afraid?"

"No, never. But this is what you've always wanted. The only reason to be afraid is if you're afraid of why he's doing it. Surely you can't doubt he loves you."

"I just don't want him to be doing it to make me happy," Ice said.

"Of course he's doing it to make you happy," Sienna said. "All men do. Do they want to be married? Probably. Do they give a damn? Probably not. But it makes you happy, so that makes them happy. Don't go analyzing it. Just go get married."

"Why? So you guys can?"

The women in the room all broke out laughing. "We're talking about it but haven't gotten any further," Sienna said. "I think we all have plans, but nobody wants to jump your gun."

"You're welcome to all go and get married," Ice said in surprise. "You know that."

"We know," Sienna said, "but you're the one who's engaged. Most of us have at least had a discussion about being engaged, but we want to see you guys happy first."

"I'm definitely not planning a group wedding," Ice said. "I just wanted something small and simple around the pool."

The women looked at each other and nodded.

As Ice walked out, an odd shift in the atmosphere occurred behind her, but she was so focused on the job at hand that she didn't really take time to understand. She thought about it briefly and then dismissed it. It didn't matter. What mattered was what was happening here right now. Because, by tomorrow, they would all be scattered and heading for Guatemala. And there was no way she wasn't going.

"Not in this lifetime," she muttered as she hopped into the elevator and dropped down to the basement level. She checked that everybody guarding the prisoners was okay and then moved out to the garage. She found the guys surrounding a huge whiteboard setup as they worked out a strategy. She stepped into place and listened. When there was a break, she mentioned ten men were on the ground in Guatemala, waiting to join up.

She saw the relief in the others. "Just as backup," she cautioned.

"That's where we like other men," Merk said. "Good job on getting hot bodies."

"They're hot and ready," she warned. "No time to lose."

"We're leaving at midnight," Levi said. "And we'll take this lot with us."

"Good. I couldn't find anyone willing to take out the garbage for us." Ice studied his face. "Are we driving? Flying? What?"

He shook his head. "We'll drive across the Mexican border with this lot, and we're taking a plane closer to Juan's compound in Guatemala."

"And?"

He looked at her steadily and said, "And you'll fly us in. We'll drop the prisoners, and we'll follow them down."

Ice thought about it, then nodded. "We'll go in heavy then," she said. "The added prisoner weight is a problem."

"We thought of that," Levi said. "But you can handle a big bird, and that's what I've got lined up."

"And who's my copilot?"

His gaze was steady and strong as he said, "If I can, it'll be me. But, if you want somebody else, say so."

She gave him a smile that she knew always broke his heart and whispered, "You're always my first choice as a copilot."

Her gaze drifted around to the others. "We're leaving at midnight. Be ready." She turned and walked out. As she went to the internal door to leave the garage, Levi called out, "Where are you going?"

"I'll measure off the drugs by weight. This drug should

also erase their memories of these last few hours, but I can't guarantee that. Regardless we want them out cold. No way I'll fight with the dozen of them once we're in a chopper."

"Are you sure you don't want to wait until we've walked them into the helicopter?" Merk asked. "How long can we keep them drugged for?"

"I'm good with thirty-six hours," she tossed back, looking at him. "How about you?"

He grinned. "I'm good with permanently, so if you want to make one of those an overdose, it won't bother me."

Ice shook her head. "They get the same chance to live as everybody else. If they pulled a gun on us here, we would have taken them out. As it was, we rounded them up. We'll drop them back home, like the garbage they are. But, if they pick up a weapon again," she said, "they're free game. They go down permanently. Absolutely no question about it." And she turned and walked away.

As she left, she heard Levi chuckle. "That's my girl."

She grinned. One thing she knew for sure: she and Levi were a matched set. Didn't matter if they walked down the aisle or not. They were meant to be together and to live or to die on that path together.

LEVI DIDN'T KNOW why Ice was holding back. He'd known since they first got together that marriage was the end game. He'd taken his time getting there, but, once here, he was in 100 percent, and he thought she would been right there with him.

No such luck.

Women. He couldn't live without her but damned if he understood her, especially lately. Then again, hormones were one thing men around the globe knew better than to face off against.

And Ice was anything but the same as other women. She could fly a helicopter into battle and be the only one to return safely. Her skills were incredible, and her second sense for her safety and those she cared for was legendary. He never bucked her intuition.

If she said pull out, they pulled out. If she canceled a mission, they might be pissed, but no one argued. She'd saved their asses too many times for that.

Yet now ... something was off. Something she was worrying about. He didn't think she was ill, but she was sleeping longer, looking more tired even with more sleep under her belt, a little more irritable. Something was up, ... and damn if he knew what it was.

And why the hell wouldn't she set a wedding date? It was what she wanted. Hell, it was what they both wanted.

So why not?

With no answer forthcoming, he headed back to take care of business.

That was at least something he understood inside and out.

Ice? ... Not so much. At least not right now.

Chapter 5

ICE WAS GEARED up and ready to go at midnight, and the convoy headed south soon afterward. They already had connections at the border, and they cleared it to get through. They were not making a normal border crossing. No way they could do that—not with a dozen unconscious men in tow. She was afraid it was a stupid idea to take them back, but the US government didn't want anything to do with them either. That was why they needed clearance to take them into Mexico. They could dump them there, but that wasn't a good choice either.

Two hours later, they pulled out onto the airstrip, where a private jet awaited them. They loaded weapons and the men on board and were taxiing within thirty minutes. Ice looked over at Levi. "We're coming to take those vehicles back home again, correct?"

He nodded. "Tomorrow night," he said, "again at midnight."

She nodded. "Good thing."

"It'll be a tight schedule. We know anything can go wrong."

"Things always go wrong. Doesn't matter. We'll deal with it."

"I hear you," Levi said. "I just wish you'd stayed home for this one."

She glanced at him. "Something extra bugging you?"

He shook his head. "Not really. It just feels off."

Ice respected his intuition. If there was one thing Levi had learned in his long and illustrious career, it was to listen to that gut instinct. Then, so had she, and her gut was talking about something completely different. "Do you think it's a trap?" she asked in a low undertone.

"Not necessarily a trap, but I think it'll be more than we expect."

"Did Bullard get back to you?"

"Yes," Levi said. "He recognizes several of our captives, and he's sending an eight-man team to Guatemala too. Said it was time he came for a visit."

She smiled at that. "That would be nice. I haven't seen him in months."

"Maybe," Levi said. "Or maybe not."

Ice understood Levi's point. Ice had a special connection between her and Bullard. But she also knew it wasn't one she would ever deepen. Not while Levi was around. Bullard needed to find somebody of his own, somebody who cared about him. It was a lonely business, and he needed to be grounded, to have a reason to come home every day. Otherwise what was the point? And sometimes that devil-may-care attitude hit you when you were out on a mission, and, if it ever did, it was just too damn easy to make a mistake or to not give a shit about the outcome. As long as she had Levi, and Levi had her, they were both promising to come home at the end of every day. Today was no different. The fact that they were both here didn't change anything. They were both going home with the rest of the team.

"With Bullard's and my contact's men, we have a lot of men on the ground as backup," Ice said suddenly.

"And we could need every last one of them, but hopefully they'll stay in the background, making sure we aren't being ambushed from behind."

Ice nodded. She was on her phone, sending messages back and forth to the office. She smiled and said, "I think the girls are planning something."

"Of course they are. Probably their own weddings." There was a snap to Levi's voice.

She ignored him. "Maybe, that'd be nice. If they got married first," she said, "we could see how they do it."

"Ha," he said. "I already saw Badger's wedding."

She lifted her head, gazed at him and said, "That was something, wasn't it?"

His gaze softened as he nodded gently. "I'm so surprised they managed to pull it off. I've never seen seven more dumbfounded men in my life."

"Or seven more absolutely thrilled men," she said quietly. "Those seven partnerships came together under some of the worst circumstances, and yet they've made the best of it. And, matter of fact, they've done way more than that. Kat's business is thriving. Her newest and best designs are unbelievable. Stone's constantly raving about them."

"He spends a fortune on his hardware," Levi said, chuckling.

"I know, but he loves it, so it's good for him."

"He also prefers to be back home these days, doesn't he?"

A smile played around her lips. "He loves technology and being the eyes in the sky, and running the command center is like being a god of his own universe. But you know as well as I do that, if you even made a suggestion that he didn't want to go in the field anymore, he'd punch you out for it."

Levi grinned. "That's the truth. The thing is, there's nobody I would rather have running command than him. He can handle all kinds of magic at once. He's saved our backs many, many times. I want him watching our backs this time too."

"Which is why I'm here"—their headsets crackled—"but nice to know you guys love me."

Ice laughed out loud. "Is everybody else asleep?"

"I doubt it," Stone said. "Bailey's been up baking. Whenever she gets worried, she gets up early in the morning and bakes."

"There are worse things to do," Ice said. "Besides, I don't think anybody'll argue with fresh bread when they get up in the morning."

"I think she's making beignets," Stone said. "The smell is killing me."

Levi looked at Ice in horror. She started to laugh. "And what do you want to bet Bailey tells Levi *too damn bad?* That he should be home where he belongs, so he could have some himself."

Stone started laughing. "Bailey is a mother hen. She wants everybody home where they belong."

"If we had a way to make that happen, we would," Levi said. "But, when the war comes home, you need to put that fire out pretty damn fast."

"That's what we're doing," Stone said calmly. "We haven't had a devastating injury or a fatality yet. We're not starting today."

Levi and Ice looked at each other and smiled. Because Stone was right. They'd run a tight ship and an efficient ship, and, so far, it had all worked. They were trying not to expand anymore, but the world had gone to hell in a handbasket, and, every time they got up, a new problem popped up somewhere that somebody had to solve. They rescued kidnap victims, took out terrorists, reclaimed hijacked ships, upended blackmailers ... It was unbelievable. Recently they'd been involved in several groups trying to topple the Argentinean government.

That had to be partly what this was all about. Governments came and went, almost on an annual basis in some of these countries. Not that Guatemala was in the same boat, but Ice had been involved as too many African countries rose and fell, depending on the boss man at the time.

Just then the pilot called out, "Descending in twenty."

She looked at Levi, but he had closed his eyes and was settling in to get a ten-minute power nap. She knew she needed to do the same, but she was too keyed up. This was a big job because it was all about saving their own asses—and about sending a message. The world needed to know that, if anybody came back to their compound, they would get their asses kicked. She glanced over at the prisoners. Just having captured them wasn't enough. Right now, absolutely no sign of life came from any of them. She'd checked their pulses as they had been moved onto the plane, and they were all just sleeping. Perfect. She closed her eyes and rested.

LEVI WAS FIRST off the plane, and he had one of the unconscious prisoners over his shoulder. Two huge panel trucks waited for them. He dumped the man in the back of the closest truck and went back for another one, while his team did the same. When the prisoners were all loaded, Levi gave the signal, and his team then loaded up in the trucks and pulled out. Two trucks on the go, heading to a different airport and a different type of bird.

This would be Ice's domain. He'd picked up a favor from the Argentinean government—one of their big Tomahawk helicopters. They'd help him out now, but they'd come calling for a return favor someday. Still, Levi needed this machine now, so he'd pay the price later. Besides, Ice was perfectly capable of flying it and was actually looking forward to it.

But Levi wasn't looking forward to anything else about this job. It all felt wrong, as if they would have the entire compound wiped out while they were away. That thought just wouldn't leave him alone. He hit his communicator and said, "Stone, make sure everything's locked down, and you keep an eye out."

"We're on it, boss," he said, strong and steady. "I know you're thinking we'll get attacked on this end, while you're out there. And it's possible, but we have more men coming in."

"There's a big gap between men coming in and men being there," Levi snapped.

"I know," Stone said. "Don't you worry. We're on it."

And with that, Levi had to be content.

Still didn't sit right.

Chapter 6

ICE SAT IN the pilot's seat. Her roaming hands went over the controls of the Tomahawk, absolutely loving to be back in a helicopter this size. She flew her own birds on a regular basis, but this was like flying a Lamborghini of the skies.

With Levi at her side and the rest of the men—good guys and bad—locked in, she started up the rotors and let everybody know they would be airborne in two minutes. She lifted the bird quietly and smoothly into the air and grinned. She glanced at Levi and said, "If you want to get me a wedding gift ..."

He snorted. "This thing is probably worth four million dollars."

"Yeah, it probably is," she said. "Actually it's probably worth ten times that." She tilted it slightly and headed toward their destination. "Are our guys attaching parachutes to the unconscious men?"

"Everybody else is taking care of business. You keep your eyes on the sky."

"I'm flying on point," she said, chuckling, as she checked out her dash. "Four missiles locked and loaded?"

"Yes, according to the instructions that we were given."

"Good," she said. She studied the dash and pointed out, "They've changed the controls for the release. Interesting. It comes with full weaponry though." She rubbed her hands together gleefully.

"Could you keep your hands on the sticks, please?"

She laughed out loud. "I feel like a two-year-old in a candy shop." She could feel the power of this machine surging through her. She'd never been more content than when she was flying—unless when in Levi's arms. But then, that was a different kind of flying too.

Tonight she soared through the darkness, loving the opportunity to do this. "No matter what happens," she said, "thank you for this."

"If anything happens," he said, "you damn well better make sure I'm with you, because if you leave me ..." He stopped, his voice breaking.

She glanced at him, worried. This was not like him. "Hey, I'm not planning on doing anything but going home healthy and happy, with you and the team."

"So you say," Levi said, "but this has all the earmarks of a bad job."

"It has all the earmarks of a job we have absolutely no choice about," she said. "They came to us. Remember that."

"I'm not likely to forget." He checked the navigation equipment. "We're less than twenty-five minutes out."

"Exactly," she said.

Just then Levi's comm crackled, and Stone's voice sounded in his ear. "Ten men in position on the ground."

"We're a little over twenty minutes out," Levi said.

"Perfect," Stone said.

"Looks like the ten men your contact promised showed up," Levi said to Ice.

"Any sign of Bullard?" Ice asked.

"He said he'd get here if he could," Levi said. "But he

was having trouble getting over from Africa so could be delayed."

"He'll be here if he can," she said.

"Maybe," Levi said. "I hope we don't need him."

"I hope not," she said, "but when we have a small army ahead of us ..."

"I know. The last intel we had was Juan had more than sixty of his own men, but we still have no idea how many are on the compound."

"Sixty is a lot," Ice said with a heavy sigh. A few more moments passed in silence, and she said, "Fifteen minutes out."

The energy was calm and quiet. Everyone knew what this job was all about. She glanced at Levi. "How are the unconscious men?"

He twisted and looked behind to see them all packed and ready to go. "They're ready."

"Good," she said. "I figure we'll open the hatch and dump them in fifteen, right before your jumps."

He sent the message to the men in the back, relaying her time frame.

She felt the controls respond with an almost intuitive kickback of what she would do before she did it. It lifted and soared and responded instantly. She shook her head in wonder. "This is magical."

"It might be," Levi said. "You're still not getting one."

"Too bad the guy we are taking out doesn't have one," she said. "I'd like that for spoils of war."

"We have to return this one, remember?"

She nodded. "Unfortunately. It would still be a great way to get a new bird," she said, sending him a sly look.

"Only if it's offered."

She groaned. "Like that'll happen. You know as well as I do that the Argentinean government won't let go of something like this."

"I don't think this Juan character has one of these anyway," Levi said. "This is cutting edge."

"Depends how much money he's throwing around. We've seen billionaires with yachts they couldn't even be bothered to go out on more than once a year."

"If Bullard arrives, he can fly too."

"That he can," Ice said, brightening. "Of course I might have to fight him for the Tomahawk. He won't want to give it back."

Levi chuckled. "You'll definitely have to fight him, but he has a soft spot for you, so he'll let you win."

"As long as he doesn't steal one we have to return. Bullard's got that edge—you never quite know if he'll walk down the right side of the law or the wrong side."

"Isn't that the truth," Levi said with a heavy sigh. "It's a good thing we know him so well."

"It is at that." She called out, "Seven minutes."

Action ensued in the back of the helicopter. Doors were opened, unconscious men were shifted. Ice could feel the weight affecting the flight. She eased up the balance a bit, her hands light on the controls. "Five minutes," she called out.

Soon she figured they were where they needed to be—flying over one of the huge expanses of perfectly groomed lawn of the great big compound down below. Even in the darkness, she could tell the difference. Huge lights lit the night.

She called out. "Now." And hovered to give her crew time to push out the twelve unconscious men.

And one by one, the men were tossed out, their parachutes pulled on the way down. She watched in her windows and mirrors as the men soared to the bottom slopes, their parachutes opening, the bodies floating gently downward. She did a complete circle and came upon their rendezvous spot.

As she lowered the bird, she knew the sound of the Tomahawk would wake people in the compound. As soon as she was low enough, the men jumped out. A vehicle waited for them, but she was staying with the bird. She looked over at Levi and ordered him, "Get your ass back here fast."

He reached over, kissed her hard and disappeared.

LEVI BOLTED TO the left, where his four men waited, then joined with the ten men on backup duty. The group split up, not a sound made as he raced toward the back corner, one of the weakest of the compound. Some of these people didn't think about engineering or about protective angles. Levi was all about the engineering. This corner had a small rise behind it that would allow him to climb over the wall much faster than it would anywhere else. He had his grappling hooks out as he took that wall on a flying leap, a jump that only gave him about twelve feet to go, and his other men were already up, over and latched on as he followed their movements. He was up and over within seconds.

He could hear a gasp from one of the other team members, who hadn't even considered this option. Not his team. His team would have known ahead of time. His men were coming down right beside him. They spread out. He had four men with him and the other ten as backups, to remain on the compound grounds, but Levi only needed his four. With him that was five, with Ice was six. He knew that, although she was standing guard at the helicopter because they needed it to get out, she was fully armed and ready. She had also landed so the helicopter and its missiles were pointed at the compound, and, if anybody thought she would hesitate to use them, they were wrong. She was deadly when it came to protecting her own.

The darkness swarmed eerily around him. There were no dogs, and Levi wondered about that. Why? Why no advanced warning system, like an animal? He had pet dogs—they were hardly security dogs yet, although they would be eventually, so maybe it was the same thing here.

Levi's compound had dogs because they had Anna, and she was forever bringing over puppies. It was deadly at his place; roly-polys were everywhere. And yet Levi was one of the first to open his arms and to hug and cuddle each and every one of them. He was expecting dogs here for some reason. They were common in Mexico.

He slipped over to the first door and tested it, but it was locked. It was also a door he didn't understand—it had some sort of mechanical lock. He motioned to Rhodes.

Rhodes stepped up. He had a small bit of C-4 he put over the lock and blew it apart. It was just a quiet little *poof,* but the door fell open.

Levi took Rhodes with him. The other three were headed to different doors.

This one revealed only a long hallway. They closed the door behind them to minimize the light. Levi waited for a long moment, but there wasn't a sound. No voices. No dogs. No security alarms. Nothing. He frowned at that.

His intel said the leader was in residence, but sometimes the intel came just before the men moved. He could hope not, but no way to tell until they did a full sweep. They moved rapidly down the hallway, using night scopes and goggles, checking out everything that moved—and, so far, nothing had.

They swept the first floor and then moved up to the next. Levi tapped his comm three times to let Stone and Ice know they were in and, so far, nothing.

He knew Ice would have her own drone checking out the sky. He kept on moving up and up and up.

When they hit the third floor and still found nothing, he caught the puzzled look from Rhodes. The rest of his men joined him.

Up ahead were two big arched doors. He motioned at his men. Two would enter, one high and one low; two would come in right behind them, and he'd take center point. As they went to open the door, it burst open, and four men came racing out, heavily armed and speaking a language nobody understood. They charged into Levi's group.

Levi took out the first one with a hard punch on the jaw that dropped him. He removed the guy's weapon and looked over to see the other armed men were down as well, without firing one shot. They quickly dragged their bodies out of the way and waited.

Gunfire soon splattered the doorway.

Levi, Rhodes, Merk, Dakota, and Brandon flattened against the wall and waited. It was silent for a moment, and then they heard harsh voices. Somebody was calling over an intercom—Levi could hear it coming from a radio on a man on the ground beside him. He reached down, picked up the device and stomped on it. There was a cry, as if that sound had burst back into someone's ear.

Levi gave a hard smile. It was now a game of cat and mouse, but not another sound was heard. Rhodes looked over at him with a question in his eyes. Levi shifted ever-so-slightly so he could look down the hallway and into the room. No sign of anyone. He crept up to the open doorway and peered around the corner.

Ice's voice on his intercom told him, "They hit the roof. They've exited the room and have gone up."

Levi swore and said, "Let's check out the room, guys, but they've gone up."

They did a search and realized a staircase led to the rooftop with no angle for them to see.

"Images coming," Ice said.

Levi lifted his phone to see the drone images. Six men surrounding one man. "Images received," he said and thought about how to get up there. "It looks like there's only one set of stairs."

"Second set of stairs on the far side," Ice said. "Directly across from where you're standing."

They bolted to the far end of the building and found another large master suite. Levi looked out the window at a deck with stairs going up to the roof. They snuck out onto the stairs, and, from the images Ice still sent from the drone, they had HVAC vents on the roof big enough to hide behind.

They crept across and lined up shots. They were almost in the clear when one of the guards saw something and pointed his gun and fired. It hit one of the rooftop pipes and made a loud *ping*. Rhodes took aim and dropped the gunman.

And now the fight was on. The gunmen spread out, trying to protect their leader, but they were picked off in no time. Swearing and cussing with his hands in the air, Juan called out, "Who are you, and what do you want?"

Levi stood slowly and said, "I want to know why the hell you thought you could come to my house and just what you thought you were after."

The man stared at him, hate in his eyes. "You're helping the Guatemalan government," he said. "Anybody who helps this government has to face me."

Levi raised his rifle and said, "That's fine. Face me then."

Just then rapid machine-gun fire came from somewhere up in the hills. Two of Levi's men took a hit, and he could feel his shoulder burn as he went down too, but not before he fired his own weapon and took out Juan, one bullet to the center of his forehead.

Juan was down, but so were two of Levi's men. Merk was swearing but alive. Rhodes worried him. He wasn't talking. Levi dragged him back into cover and saw he'd taken a bullet in the belly. He called out to Ice. "Use the drone and find that other shooter. Rhodes is down. Merk has a bullet in his arm."

"On it," she said, her voice calm and steady.

He appreciated that. He ripped off part of his T-shirt and used it to pack Rhodes's side. Thankfully he was unconscious. Levi quickly used the rest of his T-shirt to tie up the bandage, cutting off some of Rhodes's own shirt for additional packing. With that tied up and the bleeding somewhat slowed, he looked over to see Merk grinning at him.

"I'm fine," he said. "He caught my gun arm, but I'm still in fighting form."

"Whether you are not," Levi said, calm and steady, "you'll need to be."

"We got this," Merk said. "Let's go get that sniper bastard."

Chapter 7

ICE ALREADY HAD the helicopter engine started when she saw the gunmen on the roof. She'd tracked the location on the far hillside of whoever had taken down Rhodes. For that, he'd pay. With her heart sinking and blood in her eye, she punched in the power, lifted the bird and headed toward her men. She landed on the roof and, using the weapons on the chopper to give them cover fire, she started punching holes into the hillside.

With her group fully loaded, she lifted off just as a rocket launched at her. She was up and gone as it slammed into the compound, but she circled back around to come up behind whoever it was targeting her group. She dropped several more heavy rounds of ammunition on the hillside.

"He's gone," she said. "Stone, you got any satellite for us?"

"Watch your back," he said. "I'm keeping track on the ground, but that drone of yours could come in handy right now."

"I got it," Merk said. He tossed the drone out of the helicopter, letting it fall before picking up the controls and moving it away from the rotors. He allowed it to drop down lower over the ground, circling and hunting for any men still alive who had shot their group. "Somebody needs to tell the Guatemalan and Columbian governments that Juan is dead."

"I'm on that," Stone said. "But you guys need to watch it. I don't know who the hell's behind this, but somebody is still on the loose."

"Not for long," Levi said as he tapped Ice's shoulder.

She turned to look. Two men scuttled down the hillside as fast as they could. She took the helicopter directly into a nosedive, sending everyone skittering in the back. She wore a feral grin as she came down and faced the men on the cliff with the helicopter. They tried to lift and lock their weapons onto her, and she took out both of them. Then she rose up taller and asked, "Any more?"

Behind her, Levi whispered, "That's my girl."

"Find more of those assholes," she said. "Just like every ant colony, there's more where they came from."

From beside her, Merk said, "Two more there," and showed her the screen, relaying the drone's camera sending a video feed.

She nodded and took the helicopter in the opposite direction. "See if there're more," she said. As she circled around, there was no sign of anybody. The drone had picked them up on one side, but they had since disappeared. There was too much cover down below.

She glanced at Levi, and he nodded. "I'll go down," he said.

Merk beside him said, "Hell, no, you won't, at least not alone."

No time to decide. Levi hooked on and threw himself out of the helicopter as soon as they were low enough for him to make it to the ground.

Ice watched him fall, her heart in her throat, but she'd been here too many times. He'd come back to her if he possibly could. And if he couldn't ... Well, the next mission, she might just take herself out too. She didn't like that line of thinking, but it was pretty damn hard not to.

If she wasn't the only one who could fly this bird, she'd have been down there with him. She snatched the drone controls out of Merk's hand and said, "Go." But he was third in line, grabbing gear, because Brandon had already thrown himself out. With a three-man crew now on the ground, she hovered low enough where she could keep her weapons live. She had to keep an eye on her fuel too.

Dakota settled into the seat beside her and said, "Give me the drone."

She passed it to him.

Dakota was good but not as good as she was. Just something about machines in flight were her thing. She dropped down low, circling to see if she could find any movement.

And then she caught sight of him. "Uh-huh." She zoomed in so fast, even Dakota grabbed hold as she raced toward somebody hidden among the rocks. The gunman bolted for cover, and she took him out.

Dakota shook his head beside her and said, "Damn, you use this helicopter like a bloody machine gun."

"It's equipped with multiple heavy-duty machine guns," she said, her tone clear and deliberate. "And you can damn well be sure I'll use them to my advantage."

"He'll be okay, you know?"

"He bloody well better be," she said, "or else."

Dakota laughed at that. "You guys are great together," he said affectionately.

She grinned. "We've been doing this a long time. It makes you wonder if there's any point when we can't do it."

"I know," Dakota said. "I see Flynn and Anna, and I wonder myself. We've got so many men trying to help save the world. At what point do we hang up our belts and just become retired gunfighters?"

She laughed. "There was a time that you died to become a retired gunfighter. You would have made sure you went out on the job."

"Yeah, but it's different now. I'm not alone anymore."

She shot him a look and smiled. "And I think it's what keeps us coming home every day."

"Exactly."

The communication channel crackled.

"Levi?" There was no answer, just more crackling. She flew back to where she'd dropped them.

Dakota was tapping the line, trying to pick up their communication again.

She looked at him and said, "Use the drone."

He sent it over the area where they were hovering, looking to see what he could find. There was more crackling in her headset but nothing clear. She swore and dropped lower, but she didn't want to get so low that she was in line for taking a hit. If the helicopter went down, they would have a hell of a time getting back home. Not to mention paying back Argentina for the costly bird.

Just then she caught Levi's voice. "Need pickup."

"Shit." She banked the helicopter and started circling, looking for him. "Give me your location." Her voice was steady, strong and crisp.

She caught bits and pieces until finally, she heard, "... at the drop-off." She headed back to where she had dumped them, but there wasn't much clearance. She was afraid of ending up caught in the trees. She frowned, judged the distance and gave a clipped nod. She could see Levi below.

Dakota said, "Whoa, whoa, whoa, hang on a minute.

There's no room."

But she very gently and carefully lowered the huge helicopter into the small landing spot. He just looked at her as Levi and his men dashed on board.

Levi grinned and said, "Go, go, go."

Ice rose, not moving left or right but straight up, and she punched it hard, rising fast up out of the clearance of the trees. "Home?"

"Back to the airport," Levi said. "We'll meet the ground crew there."

"What about the backup group?"

"Heading home," Levi said. "Thankfully they are all intact, and we didn't need them."

She nodded and said, "Check on the wounded."

"Merk came with me, stubborn fool. And Rhodes is still unconscious," Levi said, his voice harsh.

She knew how he felt. They'd been with Rhodes since the beginning. He was one of the four who had started the company. To lose him right now ... or at any time ... Well, that would be a devastating loss, and no way in hell would she go home able to tell Sienna what had happened.

"You tell that asshole," she roared, "that he better make it through this. I won't face Sienna over it."

"I was just thinking that. How is the fuel?"

"Enough to get back to the airstrip but not much farther. We've been up and at it for an hour and a half."

"Okay, take us back to the airstrip. We'll have to land quickly."

She snorted at that. "You know that the attacks usually come from within."

"You're not thinking it'll be somebody on the ground crew, are you?"

But she left her thoughts hanging on that one. They'd find out soon enough. Grimly she flew through the early morning light, loving the sun rising to the left. It was gorgeous out, but it didn't in any way cover up the fact they were still in grave danger. At the landing site, she lowered down and called out, "We're down, but no plane in sight. I repeat, no plane in sight."

"We got that," Levi said. He opened the door, hopped out and took a look around.

Immediately he picked up his phone and called someone. She waited, the engine just gently idling as she wrestled with the idea of shutting it off.

She knew it would take precious minutes to get her back up again, and those minutes could be life-saving minutes. She could lose everybody if she wasn't ready to lift off immediately.

Instinct kept telling her to lift up, lift up, but Levi was on the ground and appeared to be unconcerned. She didn't like it. She throttled her engine. She looked at Dakota in the passenger seat and said, "Get him back on board."

Dakota dove out of the seat and screamed at Levi. He gave her a startled look, dove inside, and she punched it upward again.

Levi scrambled into the seat behind her and said, "What's wrong?"

"My gut," she said. She rose up high enough that they were out of range of anything but a missile. And, just when she wanted to tell him it was all clear, she caught sight of just that—a missile coming toward them.

She swore heavily and dropped. As long as it didn't have tracking, she'd be okay. If it had tracking, they were in for the dance of their life. She didn't have any kind of rough geographical terrain she could confuse the missile with. She moved up and to the left, then up to the right, trying to dodge it. The missile couldn't go for too long but had enough juice that it would take her out if she wasn't fast enough.

With everybody holding on for dear life, and Levi swearing a blue streak as he made call after call, she danced away from the missile. She rose, found a block of trees and dropped down behind it. The missile came right through the trees, clearing a path through the woods, but she was no longer there. She'd dropped farther down into a valley on the other side, and the missile slammed into the rocks above her. Shaky, triumphant and pissed, she turned to look at Levi. "So much for a peaceful landing."

He nodded. "Any way we can hide?"

"We can try. At the moment, I'm pretty well hidden, and the enemy doesn't know if they took me out or not."

She kept the bird hovering low as they headed down into the small valley. "At least if I'm mobile, I'm agile. But you know what happens once I stop."

He nodded. "We were set up."

"Ya think?"

He shot her a look and said, "And there's no plane waiting for us."

"I know," she said. "Now, I can take this bird far away, but I can't take it all the way home. We'll need to fuel up."

"Or we go back," he said, "back to where we were and see if we can find another way to get home."

"That's another twenty or twenty-five minutes in the wrong direction, and what are we likely to find there?"

"Another helicopter was back there."

She shook her head. "It's too small. Can't get everybody

on board. I can't travel very far with that kind of extra weight."

"How far can you get us now?"

She looked at the navigation equipment. "Maybe one hundred miles."

"I'll update the Argentinians. While I'm making calls, I can get the Guatemalan government to seize the helicopter from Juan's compound, but, without our connecting plane here, we'll have to find another way to get home from wherever we land this bird."

"While you're calling the Guatemalan government, find out what the hell happened to our pickup." She turned the helicopter and soared straight up into the sky so they could get the best loft and the best wind speed. "I'm heading home. We need a clear place close enough to the border where I can leave this helicopter for the Argentinians. But we also need to get across the border and to a good surgeon. I want Rhodes taken care of immediately."

"I know," Levi said. "You're not far now."

They flew steadily as Levi and Stone worked on the logistics. They finally came up with a landing place close to the border. They now needed a vehicle to wait for them on the other side.

"Too bad no one is home to fly one of my helos."

"I know," Levi said.

Just then a heavy booming voice filled the line. "I'll meet you at the border."

Ice cracked a grin. "Bullard, where the hell are you? I thought you would meet us down there."

"Couldn't make it. I'm actually in the air on the way to the Mexican border. I will use Stone as central and will be within visual soon."

With the two helicopters now flying together they had hope, but it was more a case of hope for Rhodes—because Ice knew perfectly well what would happen if he didn't get good medical care soon.

LEVI COULDN'T BELIEVE they'd been betrayed, but he shouldn't have been surprised. It could have been anybody ... He'd already talked to the commander he'd spoken to earlier. The commander was currently checking through the roster of men he'd sent. He promised Levi he'd have the asshole captive by morning. Levi basically told him to take care of his own place as Levi had to get the hell back home. They had an injured man on board.

At that, the commander promised to get some medical assistance, but Levi didn't trust the commander or his men anymore. "Not trying to insult you, but we look after our own. You need to clean your house before we'll trust in your men again."

The commander agreed.

Now that they were moving toward Bullard, that was good. Bullard was like Ice—he could fly like the wind. He was one of the few people Ice trusted with her own birds. He kept both a plane and a helicopter at his African compound. Made a hell of a difference when you could get the right equipment to do the job.

Levi headed back to look at Rhodes. His color was waxy and pale; the bullet was still inside, and he was still bleeding. Levi swore gently.

"Tell him to hold on. As soon as I switch over, and I'm not flying anymore," Ice said, "I can do some rough field surgery and see what we've got going on."

"That would be good," Levi said, "but I'm still afraid we won't be in time."

He heard her swear. She would hurt so badly over this. She'd blame herself, even though it had nothing to do with her. Rhodes had taken a bullet from somebody they hadn't known was out there, and, even though Ice had taken their sniper down, she would blame herself for not having done it fast enough.

It seemed like an interminable amount of time, but it was just twenty-seven minutes before they landed, the two birds coming in within minutes of each other. Levi's crew abandoned the Tomahawk with the basically empty gas tanks. They headed toward Bullard's machine. Bullard was there with the door open, and his man Ryland, one of Bullard's top men, was in the passenger side. They helped load up Rhodes and everybody else.

Bullard didn't give Ice a chance to take over. He took to the air and said, "Heading home."

"Thirty minutes to my surgical room," Ice said. She went straight to Rhodes and ripped apart his bandages, looking at the wound. "Levi, grab the medical kit." He opened it up for her and watched as she went for the tweezers. She found the bullet in the bloody mess that passed for Rhodes's gut and pulled it out. She tossed it into the lid of the metal tool kit and said, "They nicked an artery."

"You need to stabilize him."

"We need a hospital," she said. "If I was at home, I could do this but not right now."

"You can," Levi said, his voice sure, calm.

She looked at him, panic in her eyes. "It's Rhodes, Levi."

He nodded, reached out a hand, held her shoulder firm and said, "That's why you'll do it. Because it *is* Rhodes. He would understand."

Swearing, she grabbed as much gauze as she could. Clamps in hand, she cleaned up what she could of the blood pooling everywhere to stem the flow until she found the damaged artery. "Be easier if I had a straw to hold it in place so we could keep this artery open."

Levi held out a piece of plastic tubing, and Ice smiled. She gently slid it inside the delicate tissue on both open ends and clamped it down. The tube filled with blood that recirculated through his system. With that wound eased, she set about looking for more injuries. She found damaged muscle, but it looked like it was soft tissue only. No bone. The bowel had escaped being nicked, and, when she had as much cleaned up as she could, she nodded. She kept the wound open but covered with sterile gauze and turned to Bullard. "Get me home to my clinic."

"Yes, ma'am," he said with a grin. "Nice to see you too."

She laughed a real laugh, and Levi knew Rhodes now had a chance.

Chapter 8

THE RELIEF OF helping Rhodes and maybe, just maybe, giving him a chance to survive overwhelmed her. She called up to Bullard. "Damn good timing on your part. I didn't think you would make it."

"I was hoping to meet with you for the main op, but you'd already left, so I stayed with Stone to keep an eye on the compound until I could see where I was needed."

"Did you come alone, outside of Ryland?"

He snorted at that. "Hell, no. I came loaded for bear. I've got seven men with me, counting Ryland. The others are at your compound, watching."

"Watching what?" Levi asked.

"You've got a band of infiltrators coming in."

Ice sucked in her breath and stared at Levi in horror.

"That's all right," Bullard said. "We got it. Also the military stepped in, once they realized what was happening. So I think a double meet is set up. Didn't Stone fill you in?"

Instantly Stone's voice came over the comm. He coughed a couple times and said, "Um, I just might have forgotten a few details."

"God damn it, Stone," Levi swore at him.

"You needed to keep your focus, and we needed you to keep Rhodes alive. Filling your head with the rest of this shit wouldn't help," Stone said, his voice cool and also in control.

"The reason I run the command center is because I filter who needs to know what at what time."

There wasn't anything they could say to that. Rhodes was just as much a best friend to Stone as he was to Levi and Ice.

"Are we safe to land at home?" Ice asked.

"Yes," Stone said. "But I don't know that you'll have enough fuel to make it all the way back."

"I loaded up the tanks before leaving," Bullard said.

"I didn't see you do that," Stone said. "Good for you."

"We'll still have to stop and refuel," Bullard added.

"No, you won't," Ice said, trying to clean the blood off her hands, but it wouldn't come off. "Where did you stick them?"

"On the back, right beside the tank."

She nodded and stood. She put on a harness, hooked herself onto the bird, and, with the door open and Levi guiding her, she pulled herself to the fuel tanks, hooked up the extra one and started refueling.

Bullard crowed from inside. "God damn it, that's Ice."

Outside, she was grateful for doing one of the mundane jobs in her world. She'd set up a system like this a long time ago, after she'd landed in a jungle without any possibility of getting fuel, and she swore she would never run out again. She always kept extra tanks close by. Levi had helped her build a platform to keep them loaded on the helos themselves. The fact that Bullard had thought to check the fuel was huge, but then he lived the way she did. It was good for them, but it was also getting old real quick. She tried not to think about all the people back at the compound. It would be a nightmare to land this thing. If they were heading into a full-on war, it would be even worse.

With the tank refilled, she stepped inside, while still connected, and asked, "How's your gauge now?"

"We're just over half."

"That's fine," she said. "We have the other tank if we need it."

"Good enough," he said. "We should make it from here."

She just laughed, unhooked herself and said, "With any luck." She came inside, sat down and settled in for the rest of the flight.

LEVI WRAPPED AN arm around her and whispered, "He'll pull through."

She stared down at her bloody hands, now completely dried, and whispered, "So many things can go wrong."

"We've been there, all of us."

She smiled and said, "I know."

She closed her eyes, and he held her close. She crashed, her head on his shoulder, taking the moment to power down. The adrenaline rush was huge, but, when it wore off, it was done. He remembered her fighting for the fuel tanks platform to be attached to her helicopters. It was extra weight he didn't want to have to carry because it made the trips more expensive, but she had been beyond insistent about it. And he could see why now. Her forethought had saved their bacon yet again.

When they finally reached the compound, they met a drone, already in the air, looking for signs of anyone. Stone's voice crackled, "All clear."

Bullard landed the helicopter on the landing pad, and a gurney came flying toward them, the team right behind it.

Ice supervised Rhodes's removal and said, "Get him down to my surgery room."

"Oh, he'll be in your surgery room," a familiar voice said, "but you're not handling it. I am."

She looked over in surprise.

Levi started to grin. "Well, well, well, look who's here."

Ice's father, a medical doctor in his own right and a hell of a surgeon, stood with his hands on his hips as he glared at his daughter. "What kind of shit have you gotten yourself into now?"

She raised both hands in frustration. "Shit that I've been trying to get out of," she snapped. The two of them raced to the surgery room with Levi right behind them.

They ordered him out, but he refused. "I'll stand at the doorway, but I'm not leaving. Rhodes is my buddy too."

Ice's father turned to her and said, "Wash up."

She scrubbed down. They had two of the other wives on standby. One was Alina, a nurse, and Sienna, Rhodes's partner, was beside Levi. As much as she wanted to help, it wasn't a good idea.

Within seconds they had Rhodes stripped down and covered in a sheet, while her father gently worked on the open wound. They washed out the wound, and he carefully removed the piece of plastic they'd shoved inside the vein and stitched it up again. He set up an IV, looked at her and said, "Have you got blood?"

She nodded, walked over to her cooler and said, "Rhodes is O negative," and brought it to her father.

"Do you keep everybody's blood on hand?"

"Wouldn't you?" she asked, giving her father a flat stare.

Levi smirked. If there was one thing Ice would never admit to being, it was a mother hen, but there was nobody under her command she didn't look after.

Her father nodded, and they hooked up the IV line to help replace the blood Rhodes had lost. "He'll need quite a few more units," he said.

"I've got more, and I have six team members with the same blood type."

"Then keep them healthy," her father ordered. "This could get ugly."

"He's strong. He'll pull through," she said, smiling.

Levi chuckled. "Pretty sure I'm the one who told you that not very long ago," he said.

She smiled, looked down at Rhodes and said, "He'd damn well better come back, or I'll have to cross over and haul him back."

Sienna chuckled, relief in her tone, a visible easing of the tension in her shoulders. "If ever he had a reason to come back, believe me, that would do it. I know you did everything you could."

"He's coming back," Ice said. "His pulse is strong. His blood pressure is low, but we'll get that back up again. I just want to make sure no other bleeding is in there."

Her father was still rooting around inside the open wound, but he nodded and said, "It looks clean." He slowly started to stitch up Rhodes.

With that done and a fresh dressing on top, pain meds were administered, and Rhodes was covered in a clean sheet. The floor was mopped up, and then both Ice and her father washed up.

When she was finally done, with Levi standing beside her, she turned to her father and said, "I love you dearly, and your timing is perfect, but why are you here?"

Her father looked at her, his eyebrows raising.

She looked at Levi and said, "Wow, this is an interesting scenario." She glared between the two of them. "Have you got any idea?"

Levi shook his head. "No. Why?"

Her father started to laugh. "I'm not sure I should tell you," he said.

"Yes," she said, her temper prickling. She was too tired for games. "You should."

He smirked. "For your wedding."

Chapter 9

ICE WAS BACK in the office. Hiding. ... She should have
gone to her bedroom, but she was afraid of getting caught
by Levi. Instead she was at the office, trying to sort out
where they were in this war on her compound. She understood they were still in danger, and a group of men still
gathered outside. She called down to Stone. "Update."

"We're under watch," he said. "Appears to be two men
to the east and two men to the west."

"Have they moved from their position?"

"No," he said. "What's with the temper?"

"Don't ask."

"Not me," Stone said. "I'm always mild and moderate."

She laughed at that. "I suggest we have a talk with our
visitors."

"What do you have in mind?"

"A lot of men are inside now," Ice said. "I highly doubt
only those four are outside. But we need to have a talk with
them and see if they're planning on taking information back
or attacking. Right now, I'm more than ready to kick
somebody's butt."

"You could try sleeping," Stone said. "I get that Rhodes
is hurt, and I get that you feel responsible, but I highly doubt
it had anything to do with you or that you could do anything more about it."

"I don't know," she said. "He's in my sickbay right now. He's likely to pull through, although we might need more blood ..." Her voice dropped off as she reached up to rub her temple.

"You know we're always ready for that," Stone said. "You need to take a couple chill pills and relax for a bit."

"Our compound is under siege," she snapped, her anger once again rising.

"And it's under control," he said. "We're all inside. We're all safe, and now it's time to do something about the men who have us under watch."

"Why are they watching us?" she asked. "That's what I want to know."

"I think that's what we all want to know. I was expecting an attack before now. The fact that it hasn't come makes me wonder if they're waiting for more people."

"Which isn't good," she said. "Maybe they didn't get the message that their own compound is gone."

"Gone?"

"Their boss who signs their paychecks is dead. Levi took him out."

"Won't matter," Stone said. "You know that, as soon as one leader is gone, ten more are fighting for his position."

"In this case, I think a bunch of the top guys are gone. Not my problem as long as they leave us alone."

"And maybe that's what these guys are doing. They're just keeping an eye on you to see what you're up to."

"Then," she said, liking the idea more and more, "I think I'll go have a talk with them."

"Whoa, no," Stone said in alarm. "You're not going out there."

"Watch me," she said. She slammed down her comm.

She was spoiling for a fight, and she knew it. It all had to do with her father's words. The last thing she wanted was to have a surprise like that sprung on her. She and Levi had been fighting about the wedding date as it was. This was just enough to send her around the bend. She glared at the phone and realized the other two women in the office were staring at her.

She glared at them too.

They crossed their arms and raised their eyebrows.

"Why won't you guys let me intimidate you at least a little bit?" she complained in frustration but felt her temper easing at the same time.

"Because we care about you," Sienna said. "We're all in this together."

"Which is why we need to find out what the hell these guys are after."

"More to the point," Sienna said, "you need to figure out what the hell you're after."

"I don't have to figure anything out," Ice said.

"You can't blame Levi for it."

That stopped her in her tracks. She spun around, having almost reached the doorway, to look back at the women. "If he's not responsible for my father appearing for our supposed wedding, who is?"

The two women looked at each other, shrugged and said, "Basically all of us."

"What do you mean?"

Sienna explained. "We all arranged it. Because all you two do is fight about it. You might as well just get married, then you can fight as a married couple but without that big bone of contention in your relationship. So we thought we'd spring a surprise on you by bringing in your father and a minister—who's arriving tomorrow, by the way."

Ice stopped and sagged against the closest desk. "Why would you do that?" she cried out in bewilderment.

"Because you would never get there on your own," Sienna said gently. "And it's important to you. This is the one thing you've always wanted, outside of a child."

Ice hated it, but her hand instinctively went to her belly. "It doesn't matter," she said. "I've just come back from watching Rhodes take a bullet. Merk and Levi both got burned by bullets too. My father is looking at them right now."

She blew the loose tendrils of hair from her face and stared up at the ceiling. "I don't understand why you guys would think that was okay."

"*Is* okay, not *was* okay," Sienna said, her tone firm and confident. "Because we love you. We love both you and Levi, and we know this is an issue. So we wanted to arrange the wedding for you."

"And what if I wanted to arrange it myself?" Ice asked darkly.

At that, Sienna laughed uproariously. "You don't want to arrange your wedding," she said, grinning. "You'd like to have it all done, so you didn't have to worry about it. You want it perfect, but you'll never make it perfect because you have no idea how to do any of this, and that was bothering you."

Ice's jaw slowly dropped as she stared at Sienna. "Well, how did you know that was bothering me?" she demanded. "I mean, I don't do that stuff normally ..." She waved her hand, encompassing the entire office, as if that would explain anything.

Sienna still grinned at her. "I know," she said. "You

wouldn't know how to do flowers for a corsage or anything. You did a great job helping out the women in Badger's group, but *they* made all the decisions, and I know Bailey thought it was an over-the-top job. But it was absolutely phenomenal, and you were worried you couldn't do something half as nice for your own wedding because it's not your thing."

Ice crossed her arms over her chest as she stared at her friend who was also an employee. "How many are involved?"

Bailey stood, smiled and said, "All of us."

Ice shook her head. "Everybody knows?"

"Yes," Sienna said. "The only ones who didn't were you and Levi."

Her mind glommed onto that. "So Levi *wasn't* part of this?"

"No." The two women shook their heads.

She sighed gently. "I guess maybe that's one saving grace."

"I'm not sure why that would make it better in your mind," Sienna said, "because honestly that doesn't make a whole lot of sense to me. But I can see that it bothers you to think he would do this behind your back. Where, instead of doing it behind your back, he would also be trying to do it to make you happy."

Ice nodded. "And I get that," she said. "I really do. It's just a little daunting to think that everybody else was arranging all this without me."

"It's not a case of *without* you," Sienna said. "It's more *because* of you."

Her shoulders sagged at that. "I don't even know what to think anymore," she said.

"Which is why you're focusing on the men outside,"

Sienna said. "We get that we need to know why they're doing what they're doing, but, at the same time, you're focusing on that so you don't have to deal with *this*. And what we're trying to say is, *You're right. You don't have to deal with your wedding. We've got it handled.* Now, go deal with these guys and keep yourself calm because this is happening whether you like it or not."

At that, Ice jumped to her feet again and glared at Sienna.

Sienna waved her off. "Go take your temper out on somebody who wants to get his ass kicked. I have no intention of being part of it."

Ice stormed from the office, wondering how the hell she'd ended up with people so confident in what they did that they could basically tell their boss to take a hike.

Of course it had something to do with the women themselves. They were strong women to go with strong men. It was certainly eye-opening to watch how well they had made their own arrangements without her. She didn't even know what the arrangements were.

How was that a thing?

After grabbing a few hours of sleep—hoping to cool off, knowing Stone would wake her in an emergency—she headed downstairs to where many of her team were hanging around and talking to each other.

She smiled at the group and said, "I need two teams of two. We're going to have a talk with those men outside." The men nodded, all standing up. She sighed. "Not everybody here gets to go," she said. "We need to round up the men outside and keep them under guard at all times."

"They will be," one of the men said. "You can count on that."

She turned to look at the speaker, and it was Dakota. She smiled and said, "Good enough. We need two teams." She turned and looked at the others and realized she had many good men in front of her, and nobody wanted to be left out. She groaned. "I can't take you all, so what do you want to do?"

"We all want to go, but that's not working," Flynn said. "We've got men all over the place, but Dakota is here. He might as well take lead on one team, and I will take Tyson, and we'll head out two and two." He stopped, looked at her and said, "What are your plans?"

"I'll have a *talk* with the men outside. I want two men with me."

Behind her, Levi's voice said, "I'll have a talk with the other group of two outside, and I want two with me."

Ice nodded and looked at the others. "I trust the rest of you to look to Anders or Stone in the meanwhile." She glanced at several of the women clustered around. "And I need to know the minute anything happens in terms of Rhodes." She looked at Kai and frowned.

Kai stared at her, arms crossed over her chest and glaring.

"No," Ice said. "I'm not deliberately taking men to keep you here, but I need somebody inside capable of defending all the women."

Slowly Kai nodded. "Got it," she said. "Good save, by the way."

Ice shrugged. "Today I'm saying the wrong thing every time I turn around. It seems to be my day for it."

"It is what it is, as long as you realize it won't be a case of keeping us all under wraps."

"Hell no," Ice said, feeling the fatigue taking over again.

"That'll never happen. But what I do want is to make sure that we stay well balanced inside and out, from a defensive stronghold."

"Maybe," Kai said. "But you know it'll be that much more difficult to keep things here in line if it all blows up outside with you guys."

"Just make sure Rhodes and Merk are taken care of," Ice said. She turned to find Merk, supporting his bullet-grazed shoulder, still wrapped up. "What are you doing up?" she barked.

He just grinned at her. "Wanted to make sure you didn't need me outside."

"I think we got this," she said. "Kai will make sure you're kept in place too." Ice did a glaring 360 at the whole group. "Anybody who lets him come out after me knows what'll happen."

"What'll happen," Merk said in a lazy voice, "is that several men will get their asses kicked. What we want to do is make sure that nobody else comes from a different direction, so maybe what I'll do is go help Stone."

"Good idea," Ice said, "and, if the pain gets bad, you know you should go see my father."

"We got this," Merk said. "You go play cops and robbers."

"Hardly," she said.

He just laughed and disappeared. It seemed like she was still brain-fogged and completely thrown by this last twenty-four hours. That and one other thing she hadn't even allowed herself to think about ever since—and she wouldn't think about it now either. She had to deal with this first.

Levi stepped up, placed a hand on her shoulder and said, "You take your team and head out. I'll go in the opposite direction."

She nodded. "With me." She headed for her tactical gear. She was almost fully geared up, until she pulled down her bulletproof vest and realized it wouldn't be long enough. She frowned and put on a slightly larger one that came lower. Hoping nobody would notice, she grabbed two handguns and an AK-47 that she was quite happy with these days and headed down the long tunnel up to the secret hillside entrance. As soon as she stepped through the exit, the two men with her cleared the immediate area. She tapped her comm twice to let Stone know they were clear.

Stone's voice came through loud and crisp. "They haven't changed positions. Still one hundred yards to the right."

Stealthily, Ice snuck up behind them. When the men suddenly spun around, already three weapons were pointed at them. "Hello, gentlemen. I believe it's time you came inside and had a cup of coffee and a talk," she said, her voice hard.

The men looked like they wanted to take a chance with gunfire, but with odds of three to two, there would just be more bullets for each of them. They tossed down their weapons in disgust and let Ice grab them. She handcuffed their hands behind them and then secured a black bag over their heads. They were stripped of weapons and then led inside.

She put them in the general jail cell and walked away. She didn't even want to talk to them. As far as she was concerned, they were on her property, and she had the right to take them out. But it went against the grain to kill for trespassing. Still, depending on what they were up to, she didn't have a problem with it, especially as she thought about something else.

As she removed her tactical gear, making sure to keep two handguns with her, she turned to see Levi leading his two prisoners in. With all the men still hooded and in the jail cell, Ice turned to Levi and said, "Why is this full again?"

He grinned at her and said, "I guess it's a good thing we have it."

She nodded. "It speaks to the necessity for it."

"We can change our line of business," he said mildly, his gaze searching.

She shrugged and stepped back. "I don't want any part of interrogating them. But get answers one way or another." She turned her gaze to the others. "Remember. Rhodes is lying over there because of these guys," she said, with a finger pointing to her med bay, and walked out.

It had hit her while she was outside just what the hell was wrong with her—outside of the fact that she'd watched her best friend get shot, and she'd led a very dangerous mission into another part of the world that she really hadn't wanted to deal with, and now she was back again with the added surprise that her entire group had arranged her wedding which she wasn't sure she was ready for. But, at the same time, something else might be happening to her, and she wasn't sure she was ready for that either.

She walked into the kitchen, held up her hand and noticed how much it shook. She ran it under some warm water. She didn't need anybody to notice. If they ever thought she'd lost her edge, life wouldn't be the same. When her hands were clean and calmer, she leaned against the sink and stared out the window. She could see the puppies outside. They were big now, still roly-poly things. Bailey and Alfred seemed to have adopted them, but some of the others had as well.

Six total. She couldn't believe that somehow they'd ended up with six of these things.

Although, by the time they were well trained, they would end up being guard dogs for the entire compound. And that made sense to her. It was always about security. It was always about protecting her own. And it was that "her own" part that consumed her thoughts now. She was too scared to find out if her fears were real or not, but maybe—just maybe—she had one more of her own to protect than she had realized.

"Can I get you anything?" Bailey asked.

Ice dropped her head to stare down at the sink and then shook it and said, "No, I'll be fine."

Bailey put on a fresh pot of coffee and said, "No. You won't be. At least not today. Maybe not tomorrow. But when this has passed, and life calms down a little bit more, maybe you will."

"You're in on it too, aren't you?" she asked, hating that her voice was harsh and almost accusatory.

"Absolutely," Bailey said with spirit. "We love you," she said simply. "And we knew you couldn't do it on your own."

Ice turned to look at her, frowning. Bailey was an absolute wizard in the kitchen. Ice had never met a woman who was as happy to be in the kitchen as Ice was happy to be out in a helicopter. "What do you mean?"

Bailey smiled up at her. "You spend your life, all your time, defending us. Keeping us employed. Making sure the money flows. Making sure your family continues to grow with incredible speed and assurance is fine, but you keep forgetting about the one part of you that really, really isn't fine, and that's the part of you who wants to be married to Levi and to have a family," she said simply. "You'll have to take care of that last part, but you need to let the rest of us do something for you every once in a while. We've already decided what we want to do, and we want to arrange the wedding. Besides, it's too late. Everything is already arranged. I've been baking for days. So, when you get out of bed tomorrow morning, you're getting married. Honestly you should be relieved."

Ice shot her a cool look.

"You were not looking forward to planning this," Bailey said, now looking concerned, "and I want to add *whether you like it or not*, but I know that's not the way a wedding should be. You should get up in the morning rejoicing. You should get up tomorrow feeling like it's the best day of your life. That's what we all want for you. We don't want you to think you are chained to this. We don't want you to feel like you're being pressured into it, when the truth of the matter is that this *is* what you really want, but you're scared."

At that, Ice started to protest, but Bailey shook her head firmly.

"You feel like you don't deserve it and that he doesn't love you or that he loves you but he doesn't want to marry you. And you won't let yourself see the goodness of what you've created here. You won't allow those around you, who love you, to do something for you."

Ice could feel the tears choking the corner of her eyes. She leaned back against the counter and closed them, pinching the bridge of her nose, but then she heard Alfred's voice.

"Very prophetic words," he said gently. "Thank you, Bailey, for expressing that." He reached over, put his arm around Ice and said, "For once, let yourself have something for you."

She looked up at him and couldn't hold back the tears. She nodded briefly, kissed him on the cheek and said, "Yes," and then she disappeared as fast as she could. She could only hope to make it to her sanctuary before anybody saw her.

LEVI WATCHED AS she ran past him, not even seeing him at the kitchen entranceway. He looked at Bailey and Alfred, his eyebrows up. "Is she okay?"

Alfred gave him a genial smile. "She will be. Soon, and in some ways maybe not so soon, but she'll be just fine," he said gently. Bailey shot him a curious look. He just shrugged and kept a secret smile on his face.

Levi looked at him and said, "Anything I should know about?"

"You mean, besides the wedding?" Bailey said with a laugh.

"Yeah, what the hell's with that?" Levi said in amazement. "Ice and I've been fighting about it for weeks. She wouldn't let me set a date."

Bailey nodded. "We know. That's why we all got together and arranged it. Which is why her father's here and also why Bullard is here," she said with a smile.

"I don't want her to feel forced into it," Levi said abruptly. "I know she said yes, but I didn't want her to feel pushed into it."

Alfred laughed. "And she won't set a date because she doesn't think you're ready. She feels like you're being pushed into it."

Levi rolled his eyes. "I know. She tells me that on a regular basis, but it's ridiculous. I've told her over and over again it's what I want."

"So, tomorrow morning," Alfred said, "I trust you will get up, prepared to take that first step onto the next part of your life."

"Absolutely," Levi said, feeling overwhelming relief. "And thank you," he said. "I don't think it would have happened without you."

"Which," Bailey said, "is exactly why we're doing it. And it's not just me, and it's not just Alfred. Everybody's involved."

Levi shook his head in amazement. "That is incredible," he said. "I can't imagine."

"We've had fun," Bailey said. "There have been lots of secrets going on these last few weeks."

"Have you got many guests?"

"Oh, you'll see," she said. "It's been a surprise up till now, so why don't you just leave it in our hands?"

He hesitated, then nodded. "Thank you for this," he said.

Bailey shook her head. "No," she said, "thank you."

Levi looked at her curiously, and she smiled.

"You and Ice have both worked very hard at keeping us all safe and happy. You keep all of us working, doing things we want to do," she said. "We've never really had a chance to give anything back. You've both worked to keep this family functioning together in a big way. So, in the same way we just told Ice, give us a chance and let us have this opportunity to do something for you guys. I know Ice was really worried because she wanted the perfect wedding, but it's not her thing," Bailey said. "This way, ... this way, maybe it can be."

Levi smiled and said, "You know you're welcome, right?"

Bailey laughed and teased, "You know you're welcome, right, too?"

And he let out a big guffaw of laughter. "In that case, I'll go back down to the prisoners."

"You do you," she said, "just like Ice does Ice. And let us do us."

Levi lifted a hand, his spirits much lighter, and headed downstairs with a big grin on his face. The other men with him looked at him. He just shook his head and said, "I guess I have all of you to thank for this, don't I?" They all nodded. He said, "I'm a little overwhelmed."

"Wait until tomorrow," Flynn joked.

"I don't even know the details, but I know one thing. I don't want to have these guys here for my wedding day," Levi said, his hands already fisted. "So I want answers, and I want answers now," he barked.

Kai stepped in just then. "They're talking," she said smoothly. "Not very much yet, but they are talking."

"Separate them," Levi said. "Two of you take one each. We have until midnight to get this thing solved because I've got to get some sleep for tomorrow."

Levi unlocked the cell and motioned to his men to split up the prisoners. "Ten minutes apiece now. Take it as a training exercise."

It wasn't long before Brandon came back smiling and said, "They're on observation only."

"Why?"

Jace stepped in and said, "Because they want to know if you brought anything back with you, and how many of you came back and whether you left anybody alive in Guatemala."

"We did, and we didn't," he said. "Who cares?"

Kai joined them and said, "I have names for you." She held out a sheet with four names on it.

Levi looked at them and frowned. "I know these men."

She nodded. "They're generals under the current government. The coup is happening, and they want to know what side you're on."

He threw up his hands. "We've been helping whatever current government there was. I didn't know a coup was in the works until they came after us here."

"The coup that they had before wasn't under a good leader. This Juan guy was bad news."

Brandon said, "Our guy is actually thanking us for it. They needed Juan taken out, and they're grateful for your service."

Levi looked at the two of them. "So, do I understand? They wanted us to take out Juan, but now that he's gone, these four generals ..." He tapped the paper. "Are they planning to form a new government?"

Kai nodded. "And they want to know if you'll interfere or not."

"And if I don't?"

"They'll welcome you as an ally."

"And if I do want to interfere?"

"Then you become an enemy of the state," she said.

"Well, isn't it lucky that my wedding day is tomorrow, and I'm not planning on doing anything except enjoying myself," he said in exasperation. "Arrange for a drop tonight. I want these men off the property by midnight."

Chapter 10

ICE JUST WANTED to hide away. Too many people were in her office, so she ended up in her bedroom. She also didn't want to see Levi right now. She curled up in the window seat, trying to get her thoughts in line.

"Apparently tomorrow is my wedding day," she murmured. She wasn't sure how she felt about that. She didn't have a wedding dress. She hadn't had a hand in the flowers or the food—nothing. She wasn't even sure that mattered to her. The girls were right. Ice was terrified she wouldn't end up doing it as well as the other women.

She wasn't into big displays, but she wanted something meaningful. It was hard to imagine anything more meaningful than everybody getting together and arranging it for her.

But did they actually know who and what she was? She gave a small laugh. "I guess this'll tell us, won't it?" she whispered to the empty room.

In the meantime, they had to deal with the prisoners.

Slowly, her body tired and worn out, she stood, wondering if it was her age, stage of life or just the stress of the wedding issues getting to her. But she worried. She worried a lot lately. And cried easier. She walked to the bathroom and pulled out the box she'd secretly kept hidden away in the back of her drawer, and then she stuffed it back in again.

She didn't want to know.

Determinedly she walked out of her bedroom and headed downstairs to the jail facility, donning that mantle of
hardness everybody expected. As she shoved her fists into her
jeans pockets, she studied the prisoners and looked around at
the men standing guard. "Where's Levi?" she asked.

"He just went up to talk to a group in the kitchen,"
Rhodes called out from the nearby med bay.

She spun on her heels and said, "What are you doing
awake?" But she couldn't stop the delighted grin at seeing
him looking so bright-eyed and actually awake and talking.

He gave her a lopsided grin. "I love you too, kiddo."

Her heart melted. She reached out, grabbed his hand
and said, "Goddammit, we came close to losing you."

He squeezed her hand. "I'm not so easy to kill," he reminded her. "Don't go soft now."

She just glared at him. "You know we're pushing the
odds each and every time, right?"

He studied her carefully and then smiled. "Maybe it's
time you went to a desk job."

Immediately her back stiffened.

He nodded. "See? You're not quite ready to hang up
your wings, and I'm not quite ready to take off my boots and
leave them at the door," he said quietly. "We've been doing
this a long time. And, yes, at some point, one of us could
very well not come home from a mission."

"Better not *ever* happen," she said. Her fingers gripped
his so hard that she was forced to relax, so she didn't cause
him any further pain. She looked down at the dressings and
said, "Has my father been in to check on you?"

"Several times," he said cheerfully. "And I'm doing just
fine."

"Everybody is *now*," she said with a smile. "You're just

doing this so you can spend the next month and a half by the pool."

"Yep," he said. "What we need to do is find a way to keep all of those lovely world gremlins away from our gates."

"I was thinking about that. Is this because of a coup on a government we're helping?"

"Yes. And we have discussed before the sensibility of helping governments in these situations," he said. "Maybe we should take them off our list of customers."

"Maybe," she said, acknowledging the sense of that. "At least certain ones."

"Exactly. You need to get rid of those prisoners and soon."

"I'll find Levi and see what he's got planned. I want the riffraff off the property before I go to bed tonight."

Rhodes chuckled at that and then winced.

Ice reached out a hand to his shoulder and said, "You need to relax."

"I will," he said, "and, yes, I'm healing. I'll be fine."

She nodded slowly. "Maybe," she said, "but I'm not so sure that it's all good."

"It will be good if you let it," he said gently.

"You know about it too, don't you?" Her gaze searched his, and she saw the comprehension and acknowledgment. She stared down at him. "Why? Why not let us do it in our own time?"

"Because you *weren't* doing it," he said instantly, "and we didn't know what it would take to have you actually go through with it."

"What if he's not ready?" Ice murmured, unable to hold back that worry.

At that, Rhodes chuckled and then gripped her hand,

wincing. "Don't make me laugh," he said, gasping in pain.

But she stared down at him, chewing on her bottom lip.

"He's never wanted anything other than you. Put the man out of his misery."

She studied his face for a long moment and then said, "Do you really think so?"

"Don't you know that he loves you?" Rhodes asked her, his gaze searching hers.

"I know that," she said with a nod. "He always has, but he's never wanted to be tethered before."

"Times change," Rhodes said. "And we're all looking at our futures."

She nodded slowly. "I know," she said. "We were talking about maybe taking on less dangerous jobs."

"I'm all for that," he said, "especially these military ones involving foreign governments. Stop putting them on our roster. It'll keep us all healthier longer." And then he yawned.

Instantly she backed away and said, "I'll go find Levi."

"You do that, and make sure you show up tomorrow morning."

She spun on her heels, looked back at him and asked, "What time do we need to be back here?"

"At eleven," he said.

She nodded. "That's plenty of time."

And, with that, she walked out. Eleven in the morning. She thought about it and realized it really was plenty of time, and it was probably a perfect time of day for them too. In the kitchen, she poured herself a cup of coffee. Hearing voices, she found Levi standing with a group of five men. She poured him one too and walked over to hold it out to him.

He took it with a smile. "Do you want to run the helicopter tonight?"

She gave a clipped nod. "Sure. What are we doing?"

"Giving back the prisoners and getting an agreement from them that they'll leave us alone," Levi said.

"I was thinking we should probably back out of foreign government work. Rhodes and I were just talking about it."

"Yes, we've had that discussion here too," Levi said. "Stone brought it up earlier."

"Right. Guess we have to be a little more circumspect where we put our support. But, in the meantime, we have to deal with this issue now."

Levi nodded. "It's eight p.m. We're heading out in two hours."

She frowned. "Why the delay?"

"Because the other government will meet us in Mexico for the exchange."

"They could come to Texas and pick them up."

"They don't want to cross into the US."

"But do we have a free pass to cross into Mexico yet again?"

"Hence the two hours—to get it," Levi said. "If I explain what the hell's going on, I don't think they'll have a problem with it."

"Maybe they're caught in the middle anyway."

"Exactly," he said. He looked at her as the men drifted away and asked, "How are you?"

"Now that I've talked to Rhodes, much better," she admitted. "And I think he's right. We do need to stop supporting foreign governments. This coup has caught us in the middle, and this time it came back to bite us in the ass."

"I know," Levi said. "I was also thinking we should set up a perimeter farther back. It would give us more of a warning system."

"Not a bad idea. We can look at it next week." Ice reached up to rub her face. "I'll go grab some shut-eye before we head out again." Then she turned and walked away.

SHE HADN'T ONCE brought up the wedding tomorrow. He didn't know if that was a good thing or a bad thing. With Ice, one never knew. Sometimes she was the most amiable, easy-to-get-along-with person. But then something would make her balk, and you couldn't move her—no how, no way. He didn't want that to happen at the wedding tomorrow. He hadn't really understood the details until the men came to him and told him what the women were planning. Not wanting Levi to get caught by surprise, like Badger, they'd explained it all and had laid it out clearly.

Part of him wanted to just kidnap Ice and take her away to Mexico to a deserted beach, somewhere they could just be together. He had yet to think of a place to go for a honeymoon. She'd say she'd want to be right here, right now. And, since she had redone the entire backyard with a huge pool and gorgeous tropical plants and bushes everywhere, he knew he would be hard-pressed to find anything quite so nice. And, indeed, the rest of them felt the same way. It was nice to get away, but it was even nicer to come home.

He looked down to see his phone flashing with a dozen messages he had to take care of, but at the top of the list was his contact in Mexico. He answered the call, and it took only a few minutes to explain what was going on and to give them a flight plan. With that agreement in place, he stepped up the stairs just in time to meet Stone in the control room.

"You're not expecting a problem, are you?" Stone said.

Levi hesitated. "I don't want them thinking they need to send us a bigger message in case we didn't get it the first time."

Stone thought about that for a long moment and then said, "You need to double up on some firepower."

"I know," Levi said. "I was thinking of that. I was also thinking we need to take an extra man or two, but that'll increase our weight."

"The big helicopter can take it for a while," Stone said. "Make sure you get it fueled up again."

"Or we take two helicopters," he said. "I'm sure Bullard wouldn't mind."

"Actually that's a better idea," Stone said. He hit the intercom and called Bullard. Within a few minutes came a pounding on the door. Levi opened it to let in Bullard.

Bullard looked at him and said, "What's up?"

They explained the plan.

"But what are we getting in exchange?" Bullard asked.

"They're to stay away from us," Levi said. "But I'm afraid they won't want to just let us leave without giving us another lesson."

"Right," Bullard said. "So two helicopters?"

"Possibly," Levi said, "and maybe drop a team ahead of time, so we can see if they'll be honest or try to take out one of the helicopters."

"I can see them doing that," Bullard said. "Kind of a lesson like, 'Now stay out' type of thing."

"I know," Levi said. "They don't have anything of ours to give back, which is a damn good thing. But neither do we want these men. We want to give them their men back as a sign of good faith, but we also want them out of our face."

"I'll take one bird. Ice can take the other. I suggest I

leave half an hour earlier, get there first, drop my men and have everyone in position for when Ice brings you guys in and for a quick getaway afterward."

"I like that," Levi said. "Not only that you can take the extra men but getting in early …"

Bullard nodded. "I'll go check on the birds, get them fueled up and ready." He looked over at Stone and said, "Send me the flight plan, will you?"

"It's not far away," Levi said.

"Good thing," Bullard said. "You know how quickly this can go south. The sooner we're across the border and back again, the better for us."

"They have farther to come," Stone said, thinking about it. "So keep that in mind if you're thinking about going early."

"I still want to get there before them," Bullard said. "As a matter of fact, if we can be in the air in fifteen, we should. I'll take my men as backup. They'll look after me." He turned to look at Levi and said, "You'll have the four men you're taking back, plus you and Ice, and you're taking two men for backup?"

"I can't really take two," Levi said. "Weight restrictions will keep us with the four prisoners."

Bullard frowned. "And that puts our numbers in the red."

"How many have you got with you?" Levi said.

"I've got seven with me right now. I can take five," he said, "and that leaves two men here as backup against another attack."

"Good enough," Levi said. "Let's get your men up and at it right now."

He sent out a warning call, letting everybody know there was action, and action now.

Chapter 11

ICE HEARD THE signal but wasn't sure what was going on. She was back in the office, trying to get the rest of the stuff tied up. She wanted to crash at least for ten minutes but didn't think it was likely to happen. With the signal running through the compound, she was up and out the door immediately. As soon as she saw Bullard and his team, she gave him a frown. "What are you up to?"

He just gave her a lazy grin. "We're going as your back-up," he said. "But, because of that, we're going first."

As she listened to their reasoning, she nodded. "That sounds like a sensible idea. All we're trying to do is dump off their garbage."

"But we also want to be in control," Levi said. "We don't want to be unprepared and end up turning tail and running, so they think they can come and do this anytime."

"Neither do they have anything of ours we want," she said, nodding. "What we want is to be left alone."

"Exactly," Levi said. "So Bullard goes in early, sets up men to make sure we don't get double-crossed, and, if they do try anything, we can burn them right then and there and walk away."

Ice smiled. "I've pretty well had enough of being jerked around by everybody else's actions," she said in a cheerful voice, but she wondered as everybody straightened up and looked at her.

She shrugged, walked into the kitchen and said to Alfred, "I need something to eat before I head out. I was hoping to sleep, but that's not happening."

Alfred was running around cooking and baking—she had no clue what—but he had more pots and pans out than usual. She shook her head. "Forget it. I'll just grab a sandwich from the fridge." She walked to the fridge, and, as always, there were half-a-dozen stock sandwiches. She pulled out one for herself and one for Levi.

As she walked out to hand it to him, Bullard reached up, grasped it and nodded. "Thanks." He unwrapped it and took a big bite, grinning at Levi's look.

She handed hers to Levi and said, "I'll go get more."

Back in the fridge, she removed the last of the sandwiches and gave them to Bullard's men. "Remember. Nobody is allowed to get hurt," she said. "I've got one man who's just come out of surgery, and I've got two others injured. Do not piss me off by getting hurt," she warned them.

They just grinned at her. "We won't," they said in chorus.

Bullard chuckled. "They're already terrified of you, my dear. They don't need any more reminders."

Ice just rolled her eyes at him. "I mean it," she said. "No playing cowboys, and nobody comes home hurt."

"That's because tomorrow's a big day, isn't it?" he said, being typical Bullard and opening up the one topic that was being quietly avoided.

She nodded. "Apparently." She gave him half a smile and went looking for more sandwiches only to find Bailey making them. She grabbed two, put one on a plate, cut it into smaller pieces and headed down to see how her father was.

As she walked in, she saw Rhodes sound asleep, and her father waking up from his nap on the cot. He sat up and stretched. She sat beside him and said, "Are you okay?"

"I'm okay," he said, "but I would definitely feel better if my daughter wasn't going off on these midnight trips."

"I know," she said. "Might be the last one for me."

Her father scoffed at that. "You will always go if anybody's in danger, and you think you can do the job better."

"I have some up-and-coming pilots," she said, "but that's not the same thing as having fifteen years of experience at your fingertips."

"You need to take care of yourself now. You know that, right?" His gaze was deep and penetrating.

She looped her arm through his and laid her head on his shoulder. "I know," she whispered.

He dropped a kiss on her temple and said, "Can't believe you're getting married tomorrow."

"I can't either," she said with a laugh. She reached over and handed him the plate of sandwiches. "It's not much," she said, "but everybody's getting ready to leave."

He nodded. "I heard the battle call."

"Thanks for being here, Dad," she said sincerely. "I'm not sure Rhodes would have made it without you."

"You did a good job," he said. "You should have been a surgeon."

"Field surgery—about my style," she said with a laugh. "You know I'd have gotten rid of all the administrators and money guys and marketing guys in that hospital of yours. I can't stand any of that."

"I know," he said. "I can't stand them either, but they're a necessary evil. In your case, you're very gifted with that surgeon's scalpel too."

"Maybe, but a little rough around the edges," she said.

"Nothing wrong with being a bit rough around the edges," he said. He picked up a sandwich, looked at it and said, "You know what? I can't remember the last time I had a sandwich." He took a bite. His eyebrows rose, and he looked at her and said, "What on earth …"

"The sandwiches here are gourmet," she said with a smirk. "The fridge is always stocked full, so, if you ever need anything, make sure you help yourself to something."

"When you're gone," he said, "I'll get some coffee. I can't imagine trying to sleep tonight." He sighed and added, "I don't want you on my table."

She nodded. "Understood. It's the same warning I give my guys every damn time."

"Yeah," he said. "Still, you'll have to make a decision soon."

"I know," she said, refusing to go in that direction. Of course her father had most likely seen the signs even before she had. But it wasn't something she was prepared to talk about because no way was she staying home tonight. Besides, at the moment, it was a nebulous territory.

She didn't know anything for sure. She walked over to look at Rhodes, leaned down and gave him a kiss on his forehead before turning back to give her father a hug. "I've got to go gear up."

He nodded and watched as she walked away. She could feel his gaze on her shoulders as she headed out. She knew how hard it must be for him because it was damn hard for her every time Levi left. Her father had hoped she'd go into the same field as he had, and, in a way, she had, but definitely not with as much finesse.

Geared up, it was time to start her preflight. As she headed upstairs, she saw Levi standing there with the four hooded prisoners.

Ice nodded. "Do we have anybody to guard the prisoners?"

"One," Levi said, and he nodded to Brandon, standing there fully geared up.

She smiled. "Nice to have you on board this trip as you're also one of the lightest weights," she teased.

"Which is why I'm coming," Brandon said with a half laugh.

By the time they had all the prisoners secured, so they wouldn't have to worry about them during transport, she realized Bullard was long gone. "I didn't even hear him leave," she exclaimed.

"No, they went out silently in the night, as they always do," Levi said.

Ice went through her preflight operating checklist, listening for the natural rhythm of the rotors as they started up, and, when she was ready, she looked at Levi and said, "It's time."

"Let's go."

On that note, she lifted the helicopter into the air and headed through the night sky toward her destination.

"I don't like anything about this," she announced a few moments later.

"Neither do I. I'm also concerned about sabotage once we get there. It would be typical of a new government to try and take out somebody who had helped the old government."

She was glad Bullard was there ahead of them, but they hadn't heard anything since Bullard left, and that wasn't cool. As they flew toward the destination, Ice looked at him and said, "Have you had confirmation from Bullard yet?"

He shook his head. "Not yet," he said. "Let me check in with Stone."

Stone's voice filled the comm. "No communication. He's on blackout, but I've got him on satellite."

"And all is well?" Ice asked.

"All is well," he said. "They're ten minutes out from their destination."

She nodded and said, "He should have been there already, shouldn't he?"

"He wanted to be in the air in fifteen, but it was actually twenty-five. Don't worry. He gave his men some pretty good razzing about being slow."

"I highly doubt they were slow," she said. "He runs a tight ship."

"He does, at that," Stone said. "Anyway, I can't see anybody on the ground."

"What about coming up from the south?" Levi asked.

"Nothing yet."

"Are they flying in?"

"We're meeting at an airstrip, so that makes more sense."

Ice thought about it and said, "We're just inside the Mexican border though. That's a pretty old airstrip. It's not even used anymore."

"But it's still viable," Stone said. "And don't forget. We didn't set up the location—they did."

"Right." She gave a worried glance to Levi, who just nodded.

"We'll handle whatever they throw at us."

A few minutes later, Stone came online and said, "Bullard is down safe and sound. His men are spread out and in position."

She let out her breath with Levi watching her and said, "It's good to know we have backup."

He nodded and said, "Bullard is a good man."

"He is," she said neutrally. It was not a bone between them but a name. Sure, if something happened to Levi, then maybe she would go to Bullard ... eventually. It would take her a long time to get over the loss of Levi. But it also helped to know she had a friend willing to help her deal with her loss. But it wasn't something she ever wanted to experience.

She flew quietly, her senses coming alive the closer they got. "My gut doesn't like this."

"Neither does mine," Levi said. "What do you want to do?"

She frowned, thought about it and then leaned over and clicked on a few buttons, arming her weapons. She heard him suck in his breath.

"That bad?"

She nodded. "It feels that bad. I don't know what's going on, but something is."

Just then they got a communication from Bullard. "Bogey in the sky coming in from the south. Watch your back."

She nodded, dropped the helicopter to the treetops and turned to face whatever was coming. Already lined up, she locked on and fired at a rocket racing toward them. Seeing a clearing, she dropped farther down. As soon as they hit the ground, she told Levi, "Go."

The prisoners were out with Brandon and Levi holding weapons on them. Levi turned, looked back at her and said, "You stay here and wait."

"We'll see," she said. "But you know one thing for sure—I've got your back."

LEVI HATED TO leave her behind, but he had done so on missions many, many times. And seeing the missile shortly thereafter didn't help. Moving stealthily through the trees, the four prisoners at their side were not given a choice but to march forward. Gagged under their hoods, handcuffed and tied together, it was all they could do to avoid tripping in the darkness.

With them held back, Levi inched forward on his own, trying to see what exactly they were facing. This would probably turn into an absolute shitstorm very quickly, and he only had Brandon with him. He tapped his comm to make sure Bullard was standing by. When a responding tap came back, he knew Bullard was there.

"ETA?" Bullard asked.

He checked his watch. "Four minutes." He crept forward a little closer to see just what was going on at the airstrip. He saw a plane with two men standing and waiting. There was no sign of Ice, and the rest of the airfield appeared to be deserted.

As he watched, her helicopter rose in the air and came around, heading toward the airstrip. She was alone, and he had the prisoners. How the hell would that work?

She came down and landed behind the plane. He smirked at that. In case another missile was out there with the helicopter's name on it, she would make sure the plane went too. As soon as she landed, Levi and Brandon moved the prisoners forward to the edge of the airstrip. The two men from the plane headed to the helicopter. Ice hopped out with both a handgun and a rifle. The men stopped, and sharp words were exchanged. She motioned toward the plane.

Levi stepped onto the tarmac alone and called out. The men pivoted and moved toward him. He lifted the end of his rifle to hold it on them.

Their steps slowed, but they glared at him, and one man said, "Where are our men?"

Levi motioned behind him. "We've got them here."

"No double-cross," the other man snapped.

"Nope," Levi said, "no double-cross. Yet you tried to blow up our helicopter a few minutes ago. And, if it wasn't for our pilot, you would have taken us all out," he said, his voice cool, "including your own men."

Just then more men came from the far side of the plane and from inside the plane. Suddenly twenty men faced Levi, all armed. He held the rifle on the two original men in front of him, but he and Brandon were no match for the firepower they now faced.

"I thought you said no double-cross," Levi said, studying the numbers. With Bullard, they were still well ahead of the game, but it wouldn't be pretty or easy.

"We want our prisoners," one of the men snapped, as the others glared at Levi and nodded in agreement.

Levi lowered his gun and motioned for the prisoners to move forward. The prisoners walked into the group and were surrounded by their men. All four men took blows that dropped them to their knees. Levi stared, his heart sinking and his gut twisting. "Are you going to kill them?"

"They failed," the man said. "We don't accept failure here."

Levi nodded. "Got it. Where's your boss?" As he looked, one of the generals stepped from the airplane. He raised a hand in greeting and inclined his head.

"Is this the way you do business?" Levi asked.

The general smiled. "You were doing business with our government," he said, "and it's no longer the government's wish to continue said business."

"Have you successfully completed the coup?" Levi asked, half curious, half willing Bullard to be taking notes.

"We have," he said cheerfully. "Guatemala is now under military rule."

Levi backed up several steps. "Good," he said, "good luck with that."

He kept his voice neutral as he kept backing up. At his side, Brandon backed up too. Just then, all the men raised their rifles and aimed at them. Levi stopped, smiled and said, "So are you planning on killing us too?"

The general nodded. "Sorry, but we aren't leaving anybody alive who had knowledge of any of this."

"I see," Levi said, his tone neutral.

A single shot surprised them all.

But not Levi.

The men spun, looking to see where it had come from, weapons up as they scattered.

Levi watched as a red spot formed in the center of the general's forehead, and he collapsed down the airplane's steps. Soldiers raced to their fallen leader.

Helicopter rotors swirled, and Levi already knew the weapons on Ice's helicopter would be armed. He turned to Brandon and said, "Be ready."

Brandon studied his face, then looked at the helicopter, his gaze going to the weaponry, and he nodded. "Sure hope she's good with that thing."

"She's divine with that thing."

With the soldiers again surrounding them, holding up plenty of weaponry to keep them in place, Levi held up three fingers on both hands.

Three.

Two.

One.

They both dropped to the ground as machine-gun fire ripped through the air, taking out every one of the men standing close to them.

Chapter 12

ICE AND LEVI had perfected that play a long time ago, and Ice was damn glad it still worked. She couldn't be sure she had gotten them all, but she figured Levi could finish off the final few she hadn't. Besides, she wasn't done. She turned the machine guns on the plane and took aim at an engine and a fuel tank. If there was one thing she wanted to make sure of, it was that *nobody* in this group went home. This would stop here and now.

Just then, more gunfire erupted in the trees around her. She watched as Levi and Brandon hopped to their feet and ran to the trees. She swore because she really wanted them to come to her so she could pick them up, but she knew Bullard was out there with his men.

She had no idea how many others had joined in the fight. Just as she debated whether it was worth pulling back and hitting the skies again, she saw Levi and Brandon walking toward her. They were walking with six other men. They were all armed but walking relaxed. She studied the men but didn't recognize them. She reloaded her weapons, looking for a signal from Levi that he was a prisoner. Instead he reached up and gave her an okay sign plus a thumbs-up. She didn't believe him. She grabbed her rifle, stepped to the open door and pointed at the group.

Their footsteps slowed. "Ice," Levi said, "these are the

good guys."

"They're not any good guys I recognize," she said, her voice hard.

"Correct. However, the Guatemalan government still stands, and apparently we have their eternal gratitude for having taken out one problematic general."

Her mind quickly worked around what had just happened, and then she nodded. "In other words, that coup wasn't successful?"

"Exactly," he said. "And Bullard met up with them here, after Stone got hold of the government. So they'll take possession of the plane and the rest of the bodies and make sure everything here is cleaned up."

"The plane may not fly anymore," she said apologetically.

The men nodded as they studied the bullet-strewn front. "Maybe you've missed the fuel line," one of the men said hopefully.

She shrugged. "Maybe. I didn't want to use up all my ammunition."

The men nodded respectfully.

Just then she watched as another group came toward them. "Anybody hurt?" she asked Levi, keeping her gaze on the approaching group.

"Doesn't look like it." Levi glanced at the newcomers. "It's Bullard's crew coming now."

And, with a strong walk, his shoulders back, facing forward, Bullard strode rapidly toward her, his men with him. She counted everybody, looked at Bullard and said, "Everybody okay?"

He nodded. "Another half dozen in the bush aren't okay, but that's because they're all with the wrong group."

"Good," she said. "Glad to have that done with. Now let's get our asses home."

The local men stopped, looked at Levi and said, "We need to see if this plane flies."

"Have you got a pilot with you?" Ice asked.

They shook their heads. "No, looks like our pilot's injured."

"Can you fly another pilot in?"

They shook their heads.

She groaned, looked over at Levi and said, "What do you want to do?"

"We can take it back," Bullard said. "I have two pilots with me."

She glanced at him and said, "You'll be another six to eight hours then."

"I know," he said. He turned to look at his men. "Volunteers?" Four men stepped forward. He said, "Go start up the plane and see if it'll fly." They went in and got to work. Nothing remained of interest inside the plane, and then suddenly the front props turned. The plane shifted forward slightly, but it appeared to be fine. One of Bullard's men came out and said, "She'll fly just fine."

The rest of the men grinned and loaded up. Bullard looked at Ice and said, "I'll wait for my men. They'll drop them across the border. I'll follow, pick up my guys and come back."

"Fuel?"

He nodded. "I'll fuel up too."

"So you'll be back home in eight hours?"

He nodded. "Promise. Don't get married without me."

LEVI ALMOST LAUGHED at the look on her face because Bullard's last shot had brought back all the memories again. He hopped into the helicopter with Brandon and said, "Come on. Let's go home."

Ice gave him a look, but he just grinned at her. With the plane heading down the runway, and tired, weary, but grateful this was over with and that none of theirs died tonight, she turned her helicopter home. It shouldn't be too long a flight as long as the winds kept in their favor. Luckily it was a straight flight home.

By the time she finally arrived, she was exhausted. She pulled up, lowered the machine onto the landing pad and powered off the engines. She sat here for a long moment, and then Levi reached out, gripped her hand and said, "Come on. Let's go to bed."

Brandon took that moment to leave them alone.

She looked at Levi, nodded and said, "I need to prep the helicopter for next time."

"No," he said, "tonight you'll sleep."

She gave him a wan smile. "As long as we've got a team to do it in the morning. If anything happens ..."

"I'll make sure of it," he said. She smiled and scrambled to the ground. As she stood, he wrapped an arm around her for a long moment, then urged her forward.

She was so tired and dirty that, when she stepped into the shower, she didn't even hear that he was there with her. His arms went around her and just held her close. She wrapped her arms around him, laid her head against his chest, and that's how the two of them stood under the hot spray.

"Come on to bed," he said. "You're exhausted."

"I am, and I don't even know why." Wrapping a towel

around herself, she stumbled to bed, curled up under the covers and fell asleep.

Levi wondered himself. She hadn't been herself lately—tired, a little bit cranky and upset. And the wedding hadn't seemed to be the right thing to make her happy. At least not the way it had happened. It was a public issue when she had probably wanted to just go somewhere quiet and get married on their own. He hadn't even thought about that, but it was something he should have considered. With that in mind, he was getting into bed himself when Stone called.

"Problems?" he asked, walking to the intercom at the doorway.

"No," Stone said, "just checking in that all's okay. Ice looked pretty rough."

"She's tired," Levi said, studying the woman he loved as she slept deeply. "She's worn out. It's been a stressful couple days."

"I'm changing places now with Flynn," Stone said, his own voice rough. "I'm crashing myself."

"Thanks for watching our backs out there," Levi said.

"As always," Stone said, "and, just to let you know, Rhodes is doing fine too."

Levi said, "I assumed so when we didn't hear anything different. Over and out until morning."

Back in bed, he wrapped his arms around Ice and pulled her close. He whispered against her hair and said, "You need sleep. Tomorrow's your wedding day."

She murmured and mumbled something unintelligible and snuggled up against him.

He smiled and whispered to himself, "It's also your wedding day, Levi. Get some sleep."

He closed his eyes and crashed.

Chapter 13

ICE WOKE THE next morning, tired and sore. She got up, headed to the bathroom and checked her clock to realize she'd slept late. It was eight-thirty already, and Levi was still crashed beside her. Her hair was still damp from last night's shower, so she quickly braided it.

As she went to leave the washroom, she stopped, grabbed the box, pulled out the little stick and followed the instructions. She set it on the counter as she brushed her teeth and went through her morning ablutions. Keeping her eyes averted, she dressed before finally she picked it up, and her heart froze.

Positive.

She'd known inside already, but somehow she had let herself ignore the signs. But now ... Of course now she knew her father had already understood. She stuffed the stick back into the box and shoved the box right to the end of the drawer, almost numb, and definitely incapable of dealing with the news.

She walked downstairs. When she walked through the kitchen, she saw not quite a full convent of their crew but almost. She looked around, surprised to see Levi there too. "When did you get up?" she asked.

He shrugged. "You were taking too long in the bathroom, so I came straight down."

In her heart, she wondered if that was providence, giving her a lucky break, because she'd been worried about what to say to him. As it was, she wouldn't say anything. There was no privacy or time. She reached for the coffee, hesitated, and then decided a couple cups shouldn't hurt. Yet not knowing confused her. She sat down at the table and yawned.

"Late night, huh?" Stone said.

She looked at him and said, "You should know. Did you sleep at all?"

"Yes," he said, "but you need to go back up to your room and rest some more."

She stared at him, one eyebrow rising.

He nodded and grinned. "Everybody else doesn't quite know how to tell you, but you need to make yourself scarce for the next few hours."

"And how will I do that?" she asked caustically. "I don't really want to be sequestered in my room for two hours."

"Tough," Kai said.

Ice glared at her. Kai was one of those can-do, could-do and would-do-in-all-circumstances kind of person. She was a great person to have on hand in the toughest scenarios. Zoe, Harrison's partner, was the same. Ice glanced around at the faces watching her and realized all the women had come back from where they'd stayed for safe keeping, and she knew her staff. But, at the moment, Ice wasn't really in the mood.

Just then, Bailey walked in and said, "She needs breakfast first."

The trouble with Bailey was, she was soft and gentle. Everybody loved her. Just then several other women came in and sat down at the table. Ice was given stuffed croissants, scrambled eggs, and a crème fraîche dish. She looked at it in surprise, and then the men helped themselves to champagne and orange juice.

She looked at them and asked, "Mimosas for breakfast?"

"Why not?" Bailey said. "It's a special day. Can I get you one?"

"No, I'm fine, thanks." With that, Ice sat back and enjoyed the breakfast thoroughly. Well, she thoroughly enjoyed her food, but the conversation around her was pretty calm and quiet, as if they were waiting for her to leave.

She glanced at Levi. He was eating the same thing. "Feels weird when it's just the two of us eating," she announced.

"That's all right," Bailey said. "Everybody will be eating lunch."

Ice nodded and finished her breakfast. She stood, refilled her coffee cup and looked at Levi.

He nodded. "I guess we're supposed to leave?"

A group of women separated them. "Yes," Bailey said, as she led Ice back upstairs to her bedroom.

As she walked into the room, trying to figure out what she was supposed to do now, she found more of her friends and coworkers joining her, laughing and giggling. She raised her eyebrows, and they sat her down in a chair in the center of the room.

"Hair time."

"*Hair time?*" Ice said with amusement. But sure enough, her hair was taken out of the braid, and she was not allowed to see what they were doing, but out came curling irons, ribbons and all kinds of things. She stared at the feminine frippery in wide-eyed shock. Slowly, worried in spite of herself, she asked, "You won't make me look terrible, right?" She eyed all of the extra ribbons they had. "You know I don't do the ribbon thing well, right?"

"You'll be just fine," they all said, laughing.

But they wouldn't let her see anything in a mirror. She sat here with her coffee, and, when the coffee was gone, they replaced it with another glass of orange juice, after she refused the champagne, saying she was too tired for alcohol.

"You know I don't have anything to wear." It was something that had really bothered her, and yet she didn't quite know how to bring it up.

"Hair first," they said.

Ice sighed and agreed. But it wasn't just "hair." They washed it, conditioned it and then blew it dry. At the same time somebody plastered her face with gunk and called it a mask. She chuckled. "You know how normally I'd go to a spa for this."

"When was the last time you actually went to a spa?" Bailey asked with a gentle smile.

"I go sometimes," Ice protested.

Just then somebody rapped on the door and stepped in, and there were cries of "Hello, Anna."

Ice couldn't open her eyes because of the stuff they had just put on her face but muttered, "Hey, Anna."

"Well, I see you're excited."

"Nope. Trepidatious, worried, anxious, nervous, all of the above," she said with a laugh. But as she took stock of where she was inside, *what* she was inside, she realized she was happy. These women had all come together to do something for her that she had never expected, had never even thought could happen.

"I brought snacks," Anna said.

"Maybe you can pop something in my mouth then," Ice said. "Breakfast wasn't all that long ago, but these women are making me nervous." She opened her mouth, and something small was popped in.

She tasted it and said, "Still on breakfast food items, if that was bacon."

"Bacon-wrapped cheddar balls," Anna announced.

Ice chuckled. "Did you guys have anything to do with the menu?"

"Are you kidding? That's been Alfred's and Bailey's domain."

"I can't imagine you guys actually pulled together to do something like this." Just then she heard a helicopter. She straightened, and the women cried out, and she sagged back down again. "It's a helicopter," she said, as if that was the only explanation needed.

"It's Bullard coming in," Anna said. "I was just talking with Flynn about it."

"I need to know if everybody's okay," Ice said.

"No," Sienna said. "You need to remember your father's here too. So, if there's any problem, he can deal with it, and, if he needs you, he will call."

"I didn't see my father at breakfast," Ice complained.

"You'll see him soon enough," Sienna said.

Groaning at that, Ice let the women do what they would. Her hands were soaked in something special, and her feet were in a foot bath, and she slowly started to relax and to enjoy herself. "I can't remember ever doing something like this."

"Not even in college?" somebody asked. She thought it was Anna's voice but couldn't quite recognize it.

"No," Ice said. "It seems like all I've ever done is pick up machine guns and wear khakis."

"Well, today you won't be doing either of those," somebody chided her.

Ice laughed. "I will if somebody attacks the compound."

"That's not happening anymore." Another voice entered the room. She recognized a harried Louise.

"Welcome to the party," Ice said in a dry voice. "I'd say hi, but I can't even see you."

Somebody reached out and stroked her arm gently, followed by Louise's voice saying, "Hi, anyway. You look fabulous."

"That bad, huh?"

Louise went off in peals of laughter. "Absolutely that bad. But I love seeing you like this. We'll take lots of pictures and record all of it."

At that, Ice struggled upright and was finally forced back down into the chair when they all promised not to take pictures of her right now. "You're not allowed to make fun of me on my wedding day," Ice said with an authoritative voice.

"Nobody's planning on making fun of you," somebody said.

"How many are in this room now? It feels like it's completely full."

"Twelve of us already," Anna said. "And, believe me, lots more to come."

Ice smiled. "What about the puppies? Somebody decorating them for this?"

"Those *puppies*, as you call them, are pretty darn big," Anna teased. "At least they're all fixed and looking healthy. Are you sure you don't want more around here?"

Ice cried out, "No."

"Okay," Anna said, "but I'm warning you, there's always a surplus at my place."

"I know," Ice said gently. "That's one of the saddest

things, isn't it?"

"It is," Anna said. "But we've done pretty well finding homes for everybody."

Ice's feet were lifted, wrapped, then dried and placed on top of some sort of a footstool, and then something was added to her eyelids. Cucumber slices? She could feel somebody working on her toenails. "You know what? If you guys had told me that you would try to make me beautiful, I could have freed up a couple days to make that happen," she said. "No way you'll do anything with me in such a short time frame."

"Really?" Anna said. She reached over and gave Ice a gentle kiss on her forehead. "If there was any way to let the world know what a beautiful woman you were inside," she said, "nobody would even see the outside. As it is, you are an incredibly stunning woman all on your own. All we're doing is helping you to shine today."

Her words warmed Ice's heart. "You guys are just being nice to me because it's my wedding day," she said, laughing. Another tidbit of food was popped into her mouth. "What is that?"

"Miniature carrot muffin bites or something like that. Some fancy name Bailey has for them," Sienna said.

Ice chewed it carefully and said, "It's good."

"I don't think Bailey knows how to make anything that's not good," Kai said, laughing. "All I've done is gain weight since I moved here."

Ice lost track of the voices as they all chimed in.

"Right, still, it's a good place now that we have the pool. We're all out exercising on a regular basis too."

"Me too," Ice said. "I meant to get a new bathing suit, but I haven't yet. I do need to though."

"That's the problem. We're all so busy that we never take the time to find nice clothes. Most of your clothes, Ice, are work clothes."

"Of course," she said, "and we never go out for evenings, but we should be doing more evenings in. We have the lights. We have the pool now. What we should do is get some outdoor furniture set up, more tables and chairs, and have maybe movie nights or dance nights."

"Oh, I like that idea," Sienna said. "Maybe we could have like a Mexican evening or something like that."

The women were busy talking and planning, as Ice settled back, enjoying this thoroughly. It was good to hear the women all had something to say and something to offer, and they all had great ideas.

Just when Ice started to relax, her fingernails were washed off, and her hands and arms and shoulders were massaged with cream, and then the gunk on her face was washed off.

They went to work styling her hair, followed by special creams on her face. She knew she was almost done when they started on makeup.

Then came the moment. They let her look in the mirror. She looked at her face ... and her hair ... in astonishment. She was speechless. It was the look in her eyes that got her. Just that special look that said she had a secret. She wondered if any of the other women had noticed.

LEVI WAS LED outside, where he was shown all their plans. He stared in astonishment. The yard was decorated with fresh flowers and twinkle lights, and an altar was set up at one end of the pool. He looked at the glistening water and shook his head. "You guys have done an incredible amount of work here." Even as he watched, several of the women put some floating bowls in the pool, some lit candles and fresh flowers floated around the water.

He shook his head. "Ice will love this."

"Any second thoughts?" Bullard bellowed at his side.

Levi looked at him and said, "Not in this lifetime."

"Damn right, you better not have," Bullard said. "You know I'll take her away from you in a heartbeat."

"When I'm dead and gone, you're welcome to make her life as happy as you can make it," Levi said. "Until then, don't give me a reason to put you in the ground."

At that, Bullard laughed. He slapped Levi on the shoulder and said, "You're a good man. I'm jealous as hell, but she's always had you as her number one love so ..."

"Are you two done fighting?" came the much calmer voice of Ice's father.

Levi turned and grinned. "Richard, how you doing?" He reached out and shook his hand. "I can't tell you how grateful I am for your help with Rhodes."

"Ice had it well in hand," he said. "That girl would have made a very gifted surgeon, if I could have convinced her to leave you."

"Exactly what I said," Bullard said.

Levi just grinned. "What can I say? She loves me."

"I know she does," Ice's father said. "And that's why I never fought it. But you will look after my daughter, won't you?"

Levi nodded. "Of course. I always have, haven't I?" But something more was in his future father-in-law's gaze. Levi wondered what was going on. What had he missed? He said to Richard, "Did you know about this well in advance?"

He nodded. "I had a good idea of what was going on. I just didn't have a final date. When they gave it to me, you guys were in the middle of warfare as usual." He shook his head. "I spend my life putting people back together again and helping them heal, and here you guys are busy tearing them apart."

"Not quite," Levi said. "We're in the business of putting people's lives back together on a more global scale. You're on the individual details. We're on the countrywide and company-wide scale."

"And I guess both need to happen," Richard said.

Levi nodded. "They do." He looked around and said, "Did anybody here think about a suit for me?"

"We thought about the suit you wore to propose," Stone said, stepping up beside him, wearing some of the most garish Hawaiian shorts Levi had ever seen. "And then we thought maybe you wanted to go casual, like I am." He motioned at his own lack of dress, his bare chest and his blue-steel prosthetic shining in the sunlight.

Laughing, Levi shook his head. "I don't think Ice will match that look."

"Nope, she won't," Alfred said, coming out. He held up something covered in plastic and gave it to Levi. "Your tux. And all to match Ice's colors," he said. "Come on. Let's get you ready."

Levi looked around at the men, feeling choked up. Unable to trust his voice, he nodded and disappeared with Alfred. He leaned closer and said, "Has everybody been involved in this mess?"

"Everybody," Alfred confirmed. "But it's not a mess and won't be as long as we can keep the peace around here for a little longer."

"I don't even have a gift for the bride," Levi said. "That's a problem." Then panic set in. "I don't have rings either."

Alfred reached into his pocket and said, "We already contacted Diamond."

Levi took the box, stopped in the hallway and opened it. His breath caught in the back of his throat as he stared down at the ring he had designed along with Diamond to match Ice's engagement ring. He'd been desperate for a chance to give it to her, and here it was today, and they had done all this without him.

He looked at Alfred, smiled and said, "I don't know if I should be pissed I was left out of this or excited because all those details are something I no longer have to worry about."

"You're delighted," Alfred said drily. "After all the panic and worry over Badger's wedding, we decided we didn't want to deal with you too."

Levi just chuckled at that. They headed toward his bedroom, and he stopped and said, "I can't go in there, can I?"

"No." Alfred led him to one of the few spare rooms left in the place. As Levi stepped inside, Alfred told him to strip. He opened up the suit bag and pulled out a beautiful tuxedo.

Levi looked at it and said, "Isn't this a little too formal? A suit would have done."

"No," Alfred said comfortably. "A suit would not have done."

At that, Levi gave a bark of laughter and said, "As long as you say so. This isn't my field."

"No, it isn't, and we had such a hard time keeping down the number of people who wanted to come to your wedding, you know?"

"I know," Levi said. "I saw that at Badger's. They tried so hard to keep the numbers down, but it was still a lot of people."

"And we're a lot of people without bringing in very many extras," Alfred said. "But you need to be prepared. The numbers have swelled."

At that, Levi stopped. "By how much?"

Alfred shrugged. "At least triple."

"Holy crap," Levi said, running his fingers through his hair. "Are you serious?"

"Of course I'm serious." Alfred snorted. "You are both well-loved."

Levi swallowed, then pulled out a brand-new white shirt to go with the tux. As Levi shifted backward, he caught sight of a beautiful blue cummerbund. He reached over and said, "That's a gorgeous color."

Alfred smiled. "It's *Ice* blue."

Levi agreed. "Is she wearing that color?"

Alfred shrugged. "I hope she's wearing white," he said, "but I do believe this is the trim color."

With Alfred's help, Levi dressed carefully. There was just something magical about putting on a tuxedo that held so much majestic power and such a sense of pride. As he studied himself in the mirror, he shook his head. "I never would have thought."

"I know," Alfred said, and he appeared almost choked up.

Levi understood. Alfred had been more father than friend for decades. He reached out, gripped his fingers and said, "Thank you."

Alfred gave him a teary smile and then wiped his eyes impatiently. "Forgive an old man," he said, "but weddings always make me emotional."

"I'm getting pretty damn emotional myself," Levi said.

"After all this time ..."

"And you'll be gentle with her, right?" Alfred asked hurriedly.

Levi frowned, stared at him and said, "There have been a couple veiled references today that I'm not sure I understand. What's going on?"

Alfred sighed and said, "It's for Ice to tell you."

Levi had no choice but to leave it at that. With Alfred at his side, they walked down to the kitchen and outside. With so many hands helping, the backyard had been turned into an incredibly beautiful landscaped wedding reception. His best friends, the men that he'd hired and worked with, the men he trusted to guard his back and to look after his lady, had all come together with their own ladies and had created a perfect paradise for Ice.

He stood tall and straight and proud until one of the men came up and said, "Come give us a hand, will you?" Everybody was dressed in suits, and the ladies were in gorgeous dresses.

It wasn't even eleven yet, but it was obviously a big deal. He turned to look for Stone, wanting the reassurance of those gaudy Hawaiian shorts. But when Stone showed up again, his best friend wore a smile on his face and a tux on his shoulders. Levi said, "What the hell, man? I didn't even know you could look like that."

"Not only can I look like this," Stone said, "but you're not getting away without having a best man."

"There's nobody I'd rather have."

"Well, too bad," Stone said, "because you're getting three of us."

Just then Merk walked up, also dressed in a tux and a matching but slightly different-colored cummerbund. And right beside him, walking slowly with crutches, was Rhodes. He gave Levi a crooked grin. "You didn't think I would miss this, did you?"

Levi choked up as he looked at the men who had followed him into battle for years. "You know something? This is not a battle I ever thought I would win, but it still feels like I want to have the best men at my side while I forge this path. You've had my back all these years. Today is no different."

"We're no longer guarding your back," Rhodes said, with a calm carelessness that just barely showed the emotions he struggled to keep contained. "We're here to support your back. This is a day very long overdue."

Chapter 14

ICE COULDN'T BELIEVE how much fun this was. She was actually enjoying herself instead of being completely stressed and overwhelmed by all the arrangements and panicking to make her wedding perfect. Instead she was relaxed, happy and allowing all her friends to look after her. They finally had her stand up and strip down to slowly redress her, starting with brand-new silky underwear—and not a whole lot of that. She was asked to close her eyes as they gently lifted something over her head, careful to avoid her hair, and slipped it down over her shoulders. When she was finally zipped up in the back, she opened her eyes to see stunned looks on everybody around her. She looked at them and said, "Is it that bad?"

"No," Bailey said in a harsh whisper. "It's that good. You're gorgeous."

Bailey led her to the mirror on the back of the door, so Ice could see herself fully for the first time.

The Viking warrior had been transformed into a Viking princess—tall, her hair curled and hanging down in simple spirals, yet sophisticated with ice-blue ribbons braided throughout, two beautiful orchids somehow sitting off to the side behind one ear. Then her dress of white with tiny, tiny ice-blue jewels of some kind and little bits of ribbon ringlets down one side. The skirt was full but parted as she walked to show off a short ice-blue underskirt. She stood in amazement as tears collected, then ran down her cheeks.

The women rushed to her. "Oh, my God, do you hate it?" Bailey cried.

In response, Ice reached out, grabbed Bailey and hugged her hard. "It's beautiful," she bawled. "Oh, my God, it's so beautiful."

Ice had no idea that a dress like this existed. It was long and lean and flowed from her hips, giving her room to walk and to do everything she felt she would always need to do, yet she looked like the most innocent of brides. She stared at the dream look in front of her and whispered, "I can't believe it."

"Well, I hope you can," Bailey said, "because we mulled over this for a long time, trying to find something that would work. And honestly, Alfred gave us all your measurements."

"That's not something I want to dwell on," she said, laughing. "But he does order my combat clothes, so it would make sense." She slowly twirled the bottom half of the dress, causing it to flow outward, loving the tiny ice-blue panels that peeked as she moved. She said, "It's absolutely beautiful."

"Good," the women all said, standing back.

And then Ice realized half of them were getting ready to leave. "Is it time to go?" she said anxiously.

The women shook their heads and said, "We'll be back in a little bit." Six slipped out.

Ice looked over at Bailey and said, "Are you getting dressed?"

"Yes, but I have to make sure the kitchen is ready too. I'll probably be the last one," she said, laughing.

"I can't just sit here all on my own," Ice said. "That's so

not me. You know I'll go outside to see if I can help set up anything."

At that, the women still here stopped and looked at her.

"You have to promise us," Bailey said quietly, "that you *will not* leave this room until we come and get you."

Ice stared at Bailey and the others for a long moment and then slowly sank back in place. "Fine," she whispered. "I promise." At that, everybody disappeared.

As she went out, Bailey said, "I'll be back in a moment."

Finally alone for the first time in what seemed like hours, Ice got up and walked over to the mirror, where she could really take a look at the dress and her face, the makeup slightly damaged from the tears but overall ... breathtaking. Her hair was spun gold. She didn't understand how the women did it, and, even though Ice was never one to spend time worrying about looks, she looked *gorgeous.*

She was astonished and overwhelmed with joy. She turned this way and that, checking out her figure in the dress and how it would look. The room was awash in discarded papers and packages. She spent the next few minutes tidying up so that at least, when she came back after the wedding, she could get changed into something more casual.

Then she saw another dress hanging off to the side. It was short, sassy and would barely reach the bottom of her butt. It was a similar ice-blue but with white trim this time, obviously a cocktail dress for afterward.

She smiled as she held it up and whispered, "Well, guys, you really do know me." She was stunned with joy. On impulse, she picked up her phone and sent Levi a text. **I love you.**

Ice smiled as she put the phone down on the table. She needed to do that. They'd been at a lot of crosscurrents lately because she'd been out of sorts herself. With good reason. *Now that she knew.* And she would have to tell him the news sometime.

But she didn't know when. Or how. She heard vehicles arriving. The sounds outside started to swell, and she realized she had never once considered that maybe more people were coming. At the thought, her mind raced, thinking about all the extra people they could have invited and realized there could be hundreds and hundreds, depending on how far people were willing to come from. That was enough to scare her too, but she couldn't do a lot now except sit here and wait until somebody came back to free her from her room. With a smile on her face, she picked up a notepad and wrote Levi a letter.

She let all her love pour out on the page. Her fears. Her worries. Her thoughts for the future and the very important thing she needed to tell him at the bottom. She folded the sheet of paper and placed it on his pillow.

Then she realized yet something else. What about vows? Were they doing traditional vows? Were they doing nontraditional vows? She was a very nontraditional person, and so was Levi, yet in so many ways they were traditional. Now she had something new to worry about. She sat back down again, hard.

When her phone buzzed, she picked it up to see Levi had sent her a heart and the same words back. She smiled and placed her phone down. A moment later, Bailey entered with Katina, Lissa and Sienna.

"Thirty minutes," they announced, and Ice stopped and stared at them.

"Wow, those are gorgeous dresses," Ice said.

"They are," the three announced, grinning.

"You see? We all wanted to be bridesmaids, the same as everyone wanted to be best man," Sienna said. "But we chose three."

"And so, if you're okay," the other three said together, "we're your three bridesmaids to go with our best men."

Ice stared, her jaw dropping. "I didn't even think of that. I've been sitting here worrying about the vows," she said, her gaze going to Bailey, who was also dressed up in a gorgeous champagne-colored dress. She opened her arms to hug each of them in a massive group hug and said, "I'll start bawling again."

"Which is why we didn't touch up your makeup earlier," Bailey said. She brushed away her own tears and said, "You have no idea how much joy this gave us, that we could do this for you."

Ice shook her head. "I can't believe it. I seriously can't believe it. I want to run downstairs and grab Levi and race to the altar, and yet I know there's this process. I just don't know what the process is."

"I know," Bailey said, "but we have a program, and we'll go over it with you now."

At the sound of "program," Ice's heart dropped. "There's so much I don't know," she said. "There's so much I'll get wrong."

"There's nothing to get wrong," Bailey said. "The part you had to get right, you got right. You love Levi, and Levi loves you. Finished, amen."

Ice took a deep, calming breath and nodded. "That's correct," she said. "That's the most important part."

With that, Bailey sat down on the bed. With the other women listening, she went over how they would do the walk to the altar outside by the pool and then the ceremony itself with Levi. And, yes, they would do vows, but they were to be simple vows.

They would have some traditional questions and then it would be the exchanging of rings.

Ice gasped and said, "But I don't have one for Levi."

"No," they said, "but that's taken care of too."

Ice shook her head. "Oh, good Lord."

All the details she hadn't had a chance to worry about, they had taken off her shoulders. She just stared at them all in awe.

Bailey patted her knee and said, "Forget about it. It's done. When you're finally married, we've planned a huge reception for the rest of the day and the rest of the night. Then, if you and Levi want to take off tomorrow for a couple days privately, we'll make sure one of the helicopters is fully loaded and ready to go."

At that, Ice started to laugh. "That would be perfect," she said. "I have to think about a place to go."

They all nodded. "We thought of all these places. If you pick one now, we'll make arrangements so you have a room to stay in."

At the top of the list was one of her and Levi's favorite places. Ice tapped it. "That one."

"Tonight or tomorrow?"

She thought about it and said, "Tomorrow, after we get to enjoy all of today and tonight."

"Okay," Bailey said. "But we'll let them know ahead of time you might want to come in early."

"Maybe," Ice said, "but with so many of my friends here, maybe not."

"Good point." Sienna took off with the list, and Katina came over and said, "Now let's take care of that makeup."

With her eyes deliberately not on the mirror, they touched up her makeup, and, when Sienna returned a few minutes later, she said, "That's all done. The arrangements are under Levi's name."

"Good," Ice said, "and do they have a helicopter pad?"

"Ready and waiting," Sienna said, laughing.

"It's not the most common getaway vehicle," Ice said with a wry smile.

"But it's very much you," Sienna said, "so don't worry about it."

"Right," she said.

Just then a knock came at the door. Ice opened it to see Alfred standing there with her father. Ice immediately reached out to pat Alfred's arm and to mouth *Thank you.*

Her father took one look, and tears came to his eyes. "Oh, my word," he said, "you are so beautiful."

She threw her arms around his shoulders and said, "I'm so glad you are here."

"I wouldn't miss it for the world," he said. "You and Levi were always meant to be together. Now, if you're ready, we need to go down and get in position."

He wore a matching ice-blue tie to go with her colors too. She reached over, kissed him gently on the cheek and slipped her arm through his. And, with everybody surrounding her, they led the way down to the kitchen and the room off the big deck that led to the pool level. Her father said, "We're going out this way, so everybody can see."

She shook her head. "I am so nervous."

"You are," he said, "and that's good. Have you told him yet?"

She stiffened and looked at him and said, "Of course you know, don't you?"

"Sweetheart, I couldn't be happier. I've been wanting to be a grandfather for a long time."

"Levi doesn't know," she whispered, hurriedly looking around. "No one does. Hell, I barely found out for sure."

"No. But I'm sure you'll tell him soon enough."

She nodded and smiled. "Maybe tonight."

"It'd probably be a good idea to wait at least until tomorrow, I think," he said. "Enough shocks for today."

She laughed at that. In the distance, she heard the music start.

"I wonder what music they chose," she said with amusement. "I have a lot of songs I like but not that I particularly love."

"I think they decided something about you was very traditional," he said, and, sure enough, there came the wedding march.

Ice gasped and shook her head. "How can I laugh and cry at the same time?" she whispered. "I'm so confused by everything they did, and yet I'm so absolutely grateful to miss out on all those preparations."

"Here we go." The three bridesmaids arranged themselves in front with the shortest first followed by the next in height. They went down the wide set of stairs that led to the pool, and Ice watched as they headed off at the bottom with Alfred waiting and giving the timing.

As the last one went, her father leaned over and whispered, "Are you ready?"

"Yes," she whispered, "as ready as I'll ever be." And slowly they moved down the stairs and around the corner. Gasps and cheers came from hundreds of people. Her eyes flitted across the crowd in a daze. "Good Lord, how many are here?" she whispered.

"Over three hundred," her father said quietly. "You're very well-loved. You should know that."

She couldn't even see half of the faces, but she knew they were there, smiling back at her. She saw so many she knew, and damned if Badger and Kat weren't here too. Her gaze just kept flying across the guests' faces as she tried to glance anywhere but up ahead.

Finally her father squeezed her arm and said gently, "You might want to look at Levi."

She turned her gaze to see the love of her life and the man of her dreams standing at the end by the altar, waiting for her. Dressed in a tux, his colors matching hers, he stood with the three men behind, their best friends, who'd been such a big part of their lives for so long.

Perfect.

"I can't believe it," she murmured.

"Yeah, do you see the ring bearers though?" her father asked drily. "Apparently the guys have been working on that one for a long time." And there were two of the roly-poly pups, both side by side in a harness, and between them was a cushion with a ring box. The two pups slowly walked in front of her and behind the bridesmaids.

Ice could hear everybody oohing and aahing as the two puppies walked by, their tails wagging as they got up to Levi. They were ordered to come around Levi and to stand beside the minister, who she didn't recognize until she got closer and realized it was Foster, a longtime friend and her father's right-hand man. She stared at him in surprise, tears in the corner of her eyes as the man who'd been there for her and her father through thick and thin waited for her.

He smiled and said, "I'd always planned to do this."

Ice looked at Levi, and her father handed her off. As Levi's arm reached out for her, as she had so many times in the past, she reached back, grateful to know he was the only one for her.

And then the minister, one of her best and oldest friends, stepped forward and said, "We are gathered here today ..."

When the ceremony was over, the ring on her finger to match her engagement ring, and Diamond standing there as part of the crowd, Ice didn't know if she should be smiling or crying. But she was held tight against Levi as the crowd cheered. She finally stepped back a little bit to look up at him, whispering, "I never thought this day would come."

"I knew it would, just not when," he said. He kissed her gently again, then looped his arm with hers, lifted a hand to wave and walked her back down the aisle. Alfred was waiting at the other side with a glass of champagne for them. They were then led to the reception area at the pool and were engulfed by friends and family. Hours later, Levi tucked her up close and whispered, "Are you happy?"

"I couldn't be happier," she whispered.

"Well, maybe," he said, "down the road, when you have that child you always wanted in your arms. I know that's the final goal to happiness in your life."

She stopped, took the champagne from his hand and handed it off to whomever was close. Then, with everybody watching, she picked up Levi's hand and placed it on her belly. He stared at her, uncomprehending, then his jaw dropped.

She smiled and said, "Thanks for marrying me, Daddy."

And the place erupted in cheers.

Levi picked her up, twirled her around several times, then slowly, gently lowered her to her feet and kissed her passionately. She hadn't lied ...

She'd never been happier.

Epilogue

JOHAN WALKED THROUGH the compound's huge kitchen area, snagged a cinnamon bun, poured himself a cup of coffee, and walked to where a large group of Legendary Security members sat around in a circle, talking. As he took the last seat, Nico looked at him, grinned, and said, "You'll get fat if you keep eating like that."

Johan nodded sagely. "You could be right," he said, "but I'll worry about it later. These are too damn good to miss out on."

"Those are Bailey's cinnamon buns," Kai said. "They're to die for."

He munched his way through it, thoroughly enjoying the different tastes of everything here in the States. He had traveled for years in his world, decades even, but he had spent the last five years with Bullard in Africa, until he'd been sent down off the Galapagos to help rescue a science team. He'd returned with Vince to Ice and Levi's compound a week ago.

Johan was hoping to maybe do a mission here and see just how different Legendary Securities operated. He was originally from the US, but his parents had been missionaries and had traveled all over the world. Johan had gone to school in England and in Michigan. He much preferred Michigan, but school hadn't stuck with him in either place, and he'd gone on to doing trade work in Germany and then in Switzerland.

It was hard, as he looked back onto his vagabond lifestyle, to consider any particular area as home.

As he pondered the cinnamon bun along this strange path his world had taken, he heard Kai say, "I know Joy. She's not much for raising the alarm unnecessarily."

Harrison said, "*You* know Joy. We don't. She might not be one to raise alarms, but that doesn't mean that she's not a little more afraid of this being a bigger deal than it is."

Kai sank back in her chair and shrugged. "I think you're wrong."

"What did I miss out on?" Johan asked, as he took another bite of the cinnamon bun.

Kai turned to him. "A friend of mine, Joy—actually *Joyce*, but we've always called her Joy—is working at a medical research center and says drugs are missing."

"Drugs are always missing," Johan said. "I swear to God it happens in every medical center I've ever seen."

"Yes," Harrison said. "Unfortunately, in this case, it's ketamine, which is what they use to knock out horses."

"Or men," Johan said quietly. "We've had serial killers using that same drug before."

"I never thought about a serial killer," Kai said, her gaze moving around the group one by one. "And I'm definitely not mentioning *that* to Joy."

Johan chuckled. "No need to panic her. Is this just one or two bottles that everybody's worried about, or is it a much bigger issue"

"She's new there," Kai said. "And it's a large research center. They don't do any animal testing, but they're doing a lot of lab work and some of their trials are on local farm stock. They knock them out to do surgeries."

"Sounds like animal testing to me," he said, as the last bite of the cinnamon bun went into his mouth.

"I hope not," Kai said darkly. "It'd make Joy very unhappy."

"What's the difference between animal testing and this?" he asked curiously.

"I think motivation," Harrison said with a hard laugh.

"Either way," she said, "the research center has a warehouse that runs alongside a large vet clinic, and that warehouse had a lot of ketamine go missing."

"Nobody should stock a lot of ketamine," Johan said. "It's a very strong drug. You don't need very much of it. So, unless they're dealing with a huge population of bovine, equine, or, say, *elephants*"—he snorted—"I can't see anybody keeping a large stock of it."

"True enough, but they did get in a large amount, and now it's missing."

Johan stared at her, his fingers tapping his knees. His mind raced quickly as he thought about all the uses for ketamine. "If it is a serial killer, he won't need a lot of ketamine anyway. Other, more easily obtained drugs might serve him better."

"But, like you said, it's worth money on the black market," Kai said, turning to Harrison with a frown.

"Missing drugs *are* always an issue. Have they contacted the cops?"

"No. See? That's the thing," she said. "She brought it up to her boss, only he laughed at her and said she miscounted and told her to look again."

"Did she?" Johan asked, interested in the way the system worked over here.

"She did, indeed. When she went back to him with the same figures, he said it must have been an inventory error."

"Did she go to their accountant over it?"

Kai looked at Harrison and nodded. "The accountant wasn't happy, said that that stuff was expensive, but didn't confirm whether he had entered an invoice for a case of ketamine or not."

"Sounds like she's trying to do the right thing by tracking it down, only nobody else seems to care."

"I think that's a problem for a lot of large companies," she said, "because somebody'll get blamed if it did go missing."

"And is that our problem, or is this just an exercise that we're all talking about?" Johan asked.

"I'm afraid that Joy may have spoken to the wrong person and could get hurt, so I dumped it in Ice's lap," Kai confessed. "I'm not sure what she'll do with it."

A steady *clip-clip* of her footsteps coming down the hallway said they were about to find out. As Ice walked in—her hair in a long braid down her back, a simple white shirt flowing over the top of her jeans—she looked as cool, calm, and collected as ever. He'd heard that she was pregnant, but she wasn't showing much yet. She had reading glasses on, which she pulled down her nose so that she could stare over them. "I spoke to Joy," she said. "She's really worried, but her boss is apparently brushing it off."

"Yes, that's what she told me," Kai said.

Ice nodded. "However, I went above him, several rungs up the ladder, to somebody I know on the board."

"Of course you know somebody on the board," Kai said in a drawled-out voice. "Is there anybody you don't know?"

Ice flashed her a bright grin. "It helps to know a lot of

people," she said. "I just had a private conversation with him, and he's not impressed. He said, whether it was a clerical error or it's a theft, it's not a drug that they want floating around, particularly as the number for that lot has been established to come from his labs."

"Never thought of that," Kai said. "That gives more weight to getting this solved."

"Well, it should have been looked into further as soon as the issue was raised," Johan said.

Ice looked at him with interest. "You wanted a local job, right?"

He nodded immediately.

"Good. Then you and Galen can go."

At that, silence hit the gathering. Johan looked around. "And why is everybody all of a sudden staring at me that way?"

"You're not one of our regular guys," Harrison said easily. He faced Ice. "Don't you want one of us to go with them?"

"If anyone goes, it should be me," Kai protested. "Joy knows and trusts me."

Ice pondered the issue and said, "Well, I plan to send you to another job in the same area, once I get confirmation. If these guys need help, you could step up to assist them if needed."

"We don't get many jobs close to home base," Harrison said. "What's the second job? Please tell me it's something exotic, like an international jewel thief or something like that."

"Stolen African sculptures," she said.

"So then I should do the pharmacy job and their stolen drugs," Harrison protested. "Galen and Johan should do the

African sculpture job."

"Like I know anything about African sculptures," Johan joked.

Just then Galen walked into the area. He lifted a hand, walked over, and gave Ice a gentle hug. Then he headed toward Johan, tossed his bag on the floor, and dropped into a squatting position. He grinned at his old friend. "The first I realized you were here was when I found out the two of us got assigned to a job."

"Oh, yeah. She's keeping us together and away from her pretty boys," Johan said. "Everybody knows they can't handle the heat."

Galen burst into laughter. "Well, if they can't," he said, "I'm not sure anybody can." Galen stood and stretched. "Man, that's a long set of flights to get over here."

"It is, indeed," Ice said, studying him. "We just got word that our men arrived over there safely too."

"They've taken over some interesting security hardware. I wouldn't mind hearing what they're up to."

"Well, you can learn while you're here," she said. "In the meantime, Bullard wanted you to get some North American experience."

"Interesting that you're putting the two of us together," Johan said. "Both the *new* guys."

Galen rolled his eyes. "Art's not really my thing, unless shooting them up and leaving a room devastated is an art form."

"We have more than enough of that *art form* ourselves," she said in a mocking tone. "So you two will look into the ketamine theft, and, if the other job comes through, Harrison will look into the art sculpture theft. Or vice versa."

"If only the Art museum had hired us in the first place as

security," Harrison said, "this wouldn't be an issue."

"Unfortunately, yes," Ice said. "They now realize that. And as this is Kai's friend, she's going to help Johan and Galen, and if more is required I'll add Tyson to their team."

Harrison crossed his arms over his chest and nodded. "Pretty boy Tyson. He'll do just fine in a museum. Me? Not so much."

"You will," she said cheerfully, "because that's the job."

He glared at her but Johan and Galen burst out laughing. "We'll take ours. Sounds like a perfect place to start."

This concludes Book 20 of Heroes for Hire: Ice's Icing.

Read about Johan's Joy: Heroes for Hire, Book 21

Heroes for Hire: Johan's Joy (Book #21)

After helping out Vince, Johan hadn't planned on staying at Levi and Ice's compound for long. However, Johan realizes how much plans can change when Galen comes over from Africa to join Johan, and the two are sent into town on a job that's close and up-front personal to another member of Legendary Security.

Joyce, otherwise called Joy, sought a career position but accepted something out of her normal skill set in order to pay the rent. But when her inventory lists show missing drugs, she knows something ugly is going on. With no one at the company willing to listen, she turns to her old friend Kai for advice.

Johan wasn't the answer Joy was looking for, but, when she finds out the previous employee to hold her position is in the morgue, she's damn happy to have him.

Her job might be safe ... but her life? Well, that's on the line ...

Find Book 21 here!

To find out more visit Dale Mayer's website.

http://smarturl.it/DMSJohan

Bullard's Battle Series

Welcome to a new stand-alone but interconnected series from USA Today bestselling Dale Mayer. This is Bullard's story—and that of his team's. All raw, rough, incredibly capable men who have one goal: to find out who was behind the attack on their leader, before the attacker, or attackers, return to finish the job.

Stay tuned for more nonstop action as the men narrow down their suspects ... and find a way to let love back into their own empty lives.

Ryland's Reach, Book 1
Cain's Cross, Book 2
Eton's Escape, Book 3

More on this series here!
http://smarturl.it/DMBullardSeries

Turn the page for an exciting preview to Bullard's Battle.

Bullard's Battle Preview

BULLARD CHECKED THAT the helicopter was loaded with their bags and that his men were ready to leave.

He walked back one more time, his gaze on Ice. She'd never looked happier, never looked more perfect. His heart ached, but he knew she remained a caring friend and always would be. He opened his arms; she ran into them, and he held her close, whispering, "The offer still stands."

She leaned back and smiled up at him. "Maybe if and when Levi's been gone for a long enough time for me to forget," she said in all seriousness.

"That's not happening. You two, now three, will live long and happy lives together," he said, smiling down at the woman knew to be the most beautiful, inside and out. She would never be his, but he always kept a little corner of his heart open and available, in case she wanted to surprise him and to slide inside.

And then he realized she'd already been a part of his heart all this time. That was a good ten to fifteen years by now. But she kept herself in the friend category, and he understood because she and Levi, partners and now parents, were perfect together.

Bullard reached out and shook Levi's hand. "It was a hell of a blast," he said. "When you guys do a big splash, you really do a *big* splash."

Ice laughed. "A few days at home sounds perfect for me now."

"It looks great," he said, his hands on his hips as he surveyed the people in the massive pool surrounded by the palm trees, all designed and decked out by Ice. Right beside all the war machines that he heartily approved of. He grinned at her. "When are you coming over to visit?" His gaze went to Levi, raising his eyebrows back at her. "You guys should come over for a week or two or three."

"It's not a bad idea," Levi said. "We could use a long holiday, just not yet."

"That sounds familiar." Bullard grinned. "Anyway, I'm off. We'll hit the airport and then pick up the plane and head home." He added, "As always, call if you need me."

Everybody raised a hand as he returned to the helicopter and his buddy who was flying him to the airport. Ice had volunteered to shuttle him there, but he hadn't wanted to take her away from her family or to prolong the goodbye. He hopped inside, waving at everybody as the helicopter lifted. Two of his men, Ryland and Cain, were in the back seats. They always traveled with him.

Bullard would pick up the rest of his men in Australia. He stared down at the compound as he flew overhead. He preferred his compound at home, but damn they'd done a nice job here.

With everybody on the ground screaming goodbye, Bullard sailed over Houston, heading toward the airport. His two men never said a word. They all knew how he felt about Ice. But not one of them would cross that line and say anything. At least not if they expected to still have jobs.

It was one thing to fall in love with another man's woman, but another thing to fall in love with a woman who was so unique, so different, and so absolutely perfect that you knew, just knew, there was no hope of finding anybody else like her. But she and Levi had been together way before Bullard had ever met her, which made it that much more heartbreaking.

Still, he'd turned and looked forward. He had a full roster of jobs himself to focus on when he got home. Part of him was tired of the life; another part of him couldn't wait to head out on the next adventure. He managed to run everything from his command centers in one or two of his locations. He'd spent a lot of time and effort at the second one and kept a full team at both locations, yet preferred to spend most of his time at the old one. It felt more like home to him, and he'd like to be there now, but still had many more days before that could happen.

The helicopter lowered to the tarmac, he stepped out, said his goodbyes and walked across to where his private plane waited. It was one of the things that he loved, being a pilot of both helicopters and airplanes, and owning both birds himself.

That again was another way he and Ice were part of the same team, of the same mind-set. He'd been looking for another woman like Ice for himself, but no such luck. Sure, lots were around for short-term relationships, but most of them couldn't handle his lifestyle or the violence of the world that he lived in. He understood that.

The ones who did had a hard edge to them that he found difficult to live with. Bullard appreciated everybody's being alert and aware, but if there wasn't some softness in the women, they seemed to turn cold all the way through.

As he boarded his small plane, Ryland and Cain following behind, Bullard called out in his loud voice, "Let's go, slow pokes. We've got a long flight ahead of us."

The men grinned, confident Bullard was teasing, as was his usual routine during their off-hours.

"Well, we're ready, not sure about you though ..." Ryland said, smirking.

"We're waiting on you this time," Cain added with a chuckle. "Good thing you're the boss."

Bullard grinned at his two right-hand men. "Isn't that the truth?" He dropped his bags at one of the guys' feet and said, "Stow all this stuff, will you? I want to get our flight path cleared and get the hell out of here."

They'd all enjoyed the break. He tried to get over once a year to visit Ice and Levi and same in reverse. But it was time to get back to business. He started up the engines, got confirmation from the tower. They were heading to Australia for this next job. He really wanted to go straight back to Africa, but it would be a while yet. They'd refuel in Honolulu.

Ryland came in and sat down in the copilot's spot, buckled in, then asked, "You ready?"

Bullard laughed. "When have you ever known me *not* to be ready?" At that, he taxied down the runway. Before long he was up in the air, at cruising level, and heading to Hawaii. "Gotta love these views from up here," Bullard said. "This place is magical."

"It is once you get up above all the smog," he said. "Why Australia again?"

"Remember how we were supposed to check out that newest compound in Australia that I've had my eye on? Besides the alpha team is coming off that ugly job in Sydney. We'll give them a day or two of R&R then head home."

"Right. We could have some equally ugly payback on

that job."

Bullard shrugged. "That goes for most of our jobs. It's the life."

"And don't you have enough compounds to look after?"

"Yes I do, but that kid in me still looks to take over the world. Just remember that."

"Better you go home to Africa and look after your first two compounds," Ryland said.

"Maybe," Bullard admitted. "But it seems hard to not continue expanding."

"You need a partner," Ryland said abruptly. "That might ease the savage beast inside. Keep you home more."

"Well, the only one I like," he said, "is married to my best friend."

"I'm sorry about that," Ryland said quietly. "What a shit deal."

"No," Bullard said. "I came on the scene last. They were always meant to be together. Especially now they are a family."

"If you say so," Ryland said.

Bullard nodded. "Damn right, I say so."

And that set the tone for the next many hours. They landed in Hawaii, and while they fueled up everybody got off to stretch their legs by walking around outside a bit as this was a small private airstrip, not exactly full of hangars and tourists. Then they hopped back on board again for takeoff.

"I can fly," Ryland offered as they took off.

"We'll switch in a bit," Bullard said. "Surprisingly, I'm doing okay yet, but I'll let you take her down."

"Yeah, it's still a long flight," Ryland said studying the islands below. It was a stunning view of the area.

"I love the islands here. Sometimes I just wonder about

the benefit of, you know, crashing into the sea, coming up on a deserted island, and finding the simple life again," Bullard said with a laugh.

"I hear you," Ryland said. "Every once in a while, I wonder the same."

Several hours later Ryland looked up and said abruptly, "We've made good time considering we've already passed Fiji."

Bullard yawned.

"Let's switch."

Bullard smiled, nodded, and said, "Fine. I'll hand it over to you."

Just then a funny noise came from the engine on the right side.

They looked at each other, and Ryland said, "Uh-oh. That's not good news."

Boom!

And the plane exploded.

Find out about Ryland's Reach (Book 1) here!
http://smarturl.it/DMSRyland

Author's Note

Thank you for reading Ice's Icing: Heroes for Hire, Book 20! If you enjoyed the book, please take a moment and leave a short review.

Dear reader,

I love to hear from readers, and you can contact me at my website: www.dalemayer.com or at my Facebook author page. To be informed of new releases and special offers, sign up for my newsletter or follow me on BookBub. And if you are interested in joining Dale Mayer's Reader Group, here is the Facebook sign up page.
https://smarturl.it/DaleMayerFBGroup

Cheers,
Dale Mayer

Your THREE Free Books Are Waiting!

Grab your copy of SEALs of Honor Books 1 – 3 for free!

Meet Mason, Hawk and Dane. *Brave, badass warriors who serve their country with honor and love their women to the limits of life and death.*

DOWNLOAD your copy right now! Just tell me where to send it.

www.smarturl.it/DaleHonorFreeBundle

About the Author

Dale Mayer is a USA Today bestselling author best known for her Psychic Visions and Family Blood Ties series. Her contemporary romances are raw and full of passion and emotion (Second Chances, SKIN), her thrillers will keep you guessing (By Death series), and her romantic comedies will keep you giggling (It's a Dog's Life and Charmin Marvin Romantic Comedy series).

She honors the stories that come to her – and some of them are crazy and break all the rules and cross multiple genres!

To go with her fiction, she also writes nonfiction in many different fields with books available on resume writing, companion gardening and the US mortgage system. She has recently published her Career Essentials Series. All her books are available in print and ebook format.

Connect with Dale Mayer Online

Dale's Website – www.dalemayer.com
Facebook Personal – https://smarturl.it/DaleMayer
Instagram – https://smarturl.it/DaleMayerInstagram
BookBub – https://smarturl.it/DaleMayerBookbub
Facebook Fan Page – https://smarturl.it/DaleMayerFBFanPage
Goodreads – https://smarturl.it/DaleMayerGoodreads

Also by Dale Mayer

Published Adult Books:

Hathaway House

Aaron, Book 1

Brock, Book 2

Cole, Book 3

Denton, Book 4

Elliot, Book 5

Finn, Book 6

Gregory, Book 7

Heath, Book 8

Iain, Book 9

The K9 Files

Ethan, Book 1

Pierce, Book 2

Zane, Book 3

Blaze, Book 4

Lucas, Book 5

Parker, Book 6

Carter, Book 7

Lovely Lethal Gardens

Arsenic in the Azaleas, Book 1

Bones in the Begonias, Book 2

Corpse in the Carnations, Book 3

Daggers in the Dahlias, Book 4

Evidence in the Echinacea, Book 5

Footprints in the Ferns, Book 6

Gun in the Gardenias, Book 7

Handcuffs in the Heather, Book 8

Psychic Vision Series

Tuesday's Child

Hide 'n Go Seek

Maddy's Floor

Garden of Sorrow

Knock Knock...

Rare Find

Eyes to the Soul

Now You See Her

Shattered

Into the Abyss

Seeds of Malice

Eye of the Falcon

Itsy-Bitsy Spider

Unmasked

Deep Beneath

From the Ashes

Psychic Visions Books 1–3

Psychic Visions Books 4–6

Psychic Visions Books 7–9

By Death Series

Touched by Death
Haunted by Death
Chilled by Death
By Death Books 1–3

Broken Protocols – Romantic Comedy Series

Cat's Meow
Cat's Pajamas
Cat's Cradle
Cat's Claus
Broken Protocols 1-4

Broken and... Mending

Skin
Scars
Scales (of Justice)
Broken but... Mending 1-3

Glory

Genesis
Tori
Celeste
Glory Trilogy

Biker Blues

Morgan: Biker Blues, Volume 1
Cash: Biker Blues, Volume 2

SEALs of Honor

Mason: SEALs of Honor, Book 1

Hawk: SEALs of Honor, Book 2

Dane: SEALs of Honor, Book 3

Swede: SEALs of Honor, Book 4

Shadow: SEALs of Honor, Book 5

Cooper: SEALs of Honor, Book 6

Markus: SEALs of Honor, Book 7

Evan: SEALs of Honor, Book 8

Mason's Wish: SEALs of Honor, Book 9

Chase: SEALs of Honor, Book 10

Brett: SEALs of Honor, Book 11

Devlin: SEALs of Honor, Book 12

Easton: SEALs of Honor, Book 13

Ryder: SEALs of Honor, Book 14

Macklin: SEALs of Honor, Book 15

Corey: SEALs of Honor, Book 16

Warrick: SEALs of Honor, Book 17

Tanner: SEALs of Honor, Book 18

Jackson: SEALs of Honor, Book 19

Kanen: SEALs of Honor, Book 20

Nelson: SEALs of Honor, Book 21

Taylor: SEALs of Honor, Book 22

Colton: SEALs of Honor, Book 23

SEALs of Honor, Books 1–3

SEALs of Honor, Books 4–6

SEALs of Honor, Books 7–10

SEALs of Honor, Books 11–13

Heroes for Hire

Bullard's Battle Series

Ryland's Reach, Book 1

Cain's Cross, Book 2

Eton's Escape, Book 3

Garret's Gambit, Book 4

Kano's Keep, Book 5

Fallon's Flaw, Book 6

Quinn's Quest, Book 7

Bullard's Beauty, Book 8

Collections

Dare to Be You…

Dare to Love…

Dare to be Strong…

RomanceX3

Standalone Novellas

It's a Dog's Life

Riana's Revenge

Second Chances

Published Young Adult Books:

Family Blood Ties Series

Vampire in Denial

Vampire in Distress

Vampire in Design

Vampire in Deceit

Vampire in Defiance

Vampire in Conflict

Vampire in Chaos

Vampire in Crisis

Vampire in Control

Vampire in Charge

Family Blood Ties Set 1–3

Family Blood Ties Set 1–5

Family Blood Ties Set 4–6

Family Blood Ties Set 7–9

Sian's Solution, A Family Blood Ties Series Prequel
  Novelette

Design series

Dangerous Designs

Deadly Designs

Darkest Designs

Design Series Trilogy

Standalone

In Cassie's Corner

Gem Stone (a Gemma Stone Mystery)

Time Thieves

Published Non-Fiction Books:

Career Essentials

Career Essentials: The Résumé

Career Essentials: The Cover Letter

Career Essentials: The Interview

Career Essentials: 3 in 1

Made in the USA
Monee, IL
24 April 2020